THE LAST GOOD THING

J.S. JASPER

Editor: Rachel from R. A. Wright Editing

Formatter: KB. Row

For the ones that have ever felt unloved, this is for you.

"*The greatest thing you'll ever learn, is just to love and be loved in return.*"

-Nat King Cole

CHAPTER ONE

T he train crawls into the harbor station. It's always so slow that Olivia regrets getting her bags ready and standing by the door. She thinks she could step right off now and barely jog to keep up, but then she'd fall face-first into the water. So, she doesn't. (Well, that and the fact the doors are locked and she'd never do something as crazy as stepping off a moving train, even if it is going at a snail's pace.) Besides, it's nice to watch the sunlight bouncing off the waves, the seagulls swooping down to steal an unsuspecting tourist's chips, and the multitude of baskets with their overflowing flowers at the station stop.

Liv smiles to herself as she steps out of the train and the smell of the salty air hits her. The sun is shining, and the breeze is welcome, even as it blows knots into her hair. She knew she missed the sound of the waves crashing against the sea wall, but she didn't realise she'd miss the chirping of crickets in the long grass.

She's been dreading coming home. Whenever anyone from college asked if she was excited to be going back, she was never really sure. Everything about hometowns that she reads in her favorite books suggests she should be excited to be there. For the brick-lined houses and the cozy cul-de-sacs, where the flower delivery guy you know by name (despite never having had a delivery) stops you in the street to say he's missed you and "my, haven't you grown!" She should be ready for a whirlwind summer romance, or to meet a stranger on the train that happens to live close by (she didn't, thank goodness—she hates having to talk to strangers) and they appear in the same coffee shop weekly until one of them proposes marriage.

But her hometown isn't like that.

There's no one there to greet her. The only people she told she was on her way were her parents, but they were never around for her childhood, let alone picking her up from the station, so she's not shocked there's no one there to help her with her bags. (She barely has a full suitcase and an oversized beach bag, but still.) There will be no summer romance in her life. Not this time, anyway. Maybe next year, when she's moved away again.

She's not waiting for it—the love and the familiarity you get when you're in a healthy relationship. The only thing she's worried about right now is getting a job she loves. She's had one acceptance so far, for a job far, far away, and she's waiting to hear back about the other, but it's right here in her hometown, so she's not sure what's she's waiting for because she's never going to take it, but it's not like she'd close the door in its face.

It's been almost four years since she set foot here, avoiding coming back for the school breaks by taking on summer jobs and internships. The only real connection she's had from here since she left for college was when she accidentally watched an Instagram story from Noah—her annoying neighbor—and the occasional update he'd give her about her apartment.

Still. It *is* her hometown.

So, she can't wait to spend an extortionate amount of money on a punnet of strawberries from Mick's grocers, which she has to walk nine blocks to get to. She can't wait to get ice cream and dodge the seagulls as she walks along the promenade. She wants to soak up as much as she can of the sunshine and the sea before she inevitably ends up taking a job on the other side of the country. With every step she takes closer to her apartment, her heart settles. It's peaceful in a way she hadn't realized she was missing.

"Hey!" a driver screams out their open car window. "Get out of my fucking lane!"

Olivia pulls her lip between her teeth to avoid smiling to herself in the street for a second time in two minutes, but it slips through just a little.

She's not mad about being back.

Olivia wants to go back to college, and she's only been walking for eight minutes and thirty-four seconds (enough time to replay her favorite summer song two and a half times). She's contemplating stopping in the street to pull her phone out so she can look up when the next train is. She's barely halfway to her apartment, but somehow, in the four years she hasn't been here, she forgot how lonely this town made her feel, and all she really needed to see to be reminded was the white and green ferryboats.

She thinks it's a little sad, actually, to still be avoiding the ferry because her dad said he'd take her for her sixth, eighth, ninth, and twelfth birthday but never did. She's twenty-three now, so she could go on the ferry alone if she wanted. She wouldn't even need a reason—no one would ask where she was going if she bought a return ticket. She could just sit on the top deck and sketch the skyline. She wouldn't even need to get off. She could sit in the middle of the old life-rafts-turned-seats and look at the clouds while her feet never touched the ground.

But the thought of buying a ticket and walking along the pontoon and sitting on the top deck all by herself on a single seat (she'd never actually take up a group space on her own, she's not a savage) reminds her of how her parents always let her down, and how alone she really is. How alone she's always been.

As she walks past the hordes of families on summer vacation, she remembers how she used to get dressed every morning when it was sunny. She'd put on a summer dress and pack a bag and she'd wait in the kitchen for one of her parents to offer to take her out. Olivia never wanted to go anywhere expensive (though her parents could have afforded it, it's all they ever spoke about—buying another rental property or financing a new car that Olivia saw the inside of less than a handful of times). She only ever wanted to go to the park or try and get a hotdog without being attacked by seagulls. Or maybe just sit in the house together doing nothing.

But her parents were always too busy, and she was too young to understand anything apart from the fact they weren't around.

Parents have to work; she knew that. She'd reasoned at a young age that to provide things like clothes for school and food in the fridge she'd have to sacrifice some of the time she spent with either her mother or father.

She just didn't think it would be both of them, and all of the time. She's not sure they wanted a child at all. It seemed to be more what they did because it was what they thought they were supposed to do.

But Olivia doesn't want to blame her parents for that anymore—for not being there for her when she was younger. According to her best friend Steph, it's "a process." A process that sounds dull and upsetting, if she has to think about it. She wants to be over it right now, but she gathers it'll hit her full force when she gets back to her apartment and it's empty.

CHAPTER TWO

The apartment building looks the same from the outside. She shouldn't be surprised. Olivia thinks she would have been told if it had burned down. The reddish-brown bricks of the walls and the fire escape that threatens to fall with every passing second remain unchanged. From the outside, her bedroom window looks like every other window. The curtains are up and the glass slightly smeared from the window cleaners that come once a month. From the outside, you wouldn't know the place has been abandoned for four years. You wouldn't know how that room is the only place where Olivia feels any resemblance to home.

"Hey, Livvie!"

Olivia looks around, a smile blossoming on her face as she recognizes the voice and the happiness of Oscar, the man who owns the hot food truck currently parked on the other side of the road. Every Thursday after school, Olivia and Noah—the bane of her existence who just *had* to go to the same school as her (he said it wasn't his fault, it's the way the district works, but she wouldn't put it past him to be difficult on purpose)—would go to Oscar for two meat-filled tacos and two that were just cheese and pico de gallo. (Yes, she missed them when she was at college, but only the food and not the stomach pains from eating that much dairy when she's eighty percent sure she's at least a little lactose intolerant.)

Oscar also gave her free tacos sometimes after he closed his truck. She wanted to boast about it to Noah, but she's pretty sure Oscar gave them to him too.

"Hey, Ossie," Liv replies with a wave. She won't go over right now. He has a line of five customers, and he's the type to get distracted and talk to her instead of feeding the people in the queue. Luckily for him, he's charming enough for people to let it slide.

Her smile lingers at the corners of her mouth, even as she has to press the button for her floor three times before the lift moves. Maybe coming back won't be the worst thing after all.

The lift shudders to a stop on the fourth floor, and it makes her jump, even if she was expecting it. Olivia has never been sure why Paul, the superintendent, doesn't fix the lift. The apartment building is nice. Nothing is ridiculously creaky, nothing appears to be growing mold, and all the lights work (a step up from college accommodation), so she's not sure why Paul is letting the first impression of the building be—well, yeah, you might fall to your death in this lift. Bye!

The intrusive thoughts wedge behind her eyes as she walks up to her front door. The key slides in with no resistance. Well, at least the lock hasn't seized. Liv gathers Helen next door—Noah's mom, the best woman in the world, probably—still has her key and has still been checking in on the place. It's something Helen had said she would do from the moment Liv mentioned going to college hours away. Helen was always looking out for her, either inviting her over when she had an evening alone or turning up in the morning before school with breakfast. Liv wouldn't say Helen raised her, but she certainly wouldn't be alive today if Helen and her husband Joe hadn't been around.

Liv's parents still own the apartment; that much she knows by the mortgage statements that come through the post. Noah would give her a rundown of the post that came through every couple of weeks (mortgage statements, beauty vouchers, and her high school diploma that was folded in half even with the large "fragile" sticker on the front). She decided before she moved out that she should be aware if they'd sold the place, because even if coming back here was the last thing she wanted to do, it was still an possibility. (One she didn't take for the entirety of college, but now there's a graphic design job she might want here, so she's weighing up her options.)

Even though the mortgage payments have been made, Liv would be surprised if either of her parents had been in it once in the entire four years she's been away.

Still, when she walks in, there's a part of her that still expects to see them. Deep inside her chest, she thinks that maybe they miss her as well. Maybe her mom would be sitting on the sofa reading a book, and maybe her dad would be making a cup of tea while swaying to a record in the background.

They aren't, obviously. Liv isn't even sure what either of them like to do in their free time now, what they do to relax when they're at home. She's not even sure where their home is.

She doesn't dwell on it.

The sofas are in the same position, the cushions plumped because no one has been sitting on them. To be fair, they looked a lot like that when Olivia did live here—she used to spend most of her time in her bedroom or Noah's room anyway. The coffee table remains an eyesore, far too big for the space, but she never wanted to redecorate the apartment. It's not hers. Her parents told her she could have creative control because they were just "so busy with work," which meant they wouldn't have noticed if she painted the entire thing green and pink. After all, they were never around. She does think that green would look nice, though. She's into natural tones right now.

Thankfully, there is no smell coming from anywhere, so she assumes she did remember to take all the food from the fridge. She did text Noah the night she got to college to ask him to double-check, because he had a house key, and he replied he "couldn't check right now because he's having an orgy in her bed, but he'll check on the way out." Olivia was sixty-seven percent sure he was joking. Not concerned enough to get on a train and figure it out, though.

But when she enters her bedroom, her chest feels calmer. Her bedroom is the only place in this apartment that was ever truly hers. Her double bed remains where it's always been, the white sheets fluffy on top. Her desk is remarkably dust free, the books she couldn't take with her still lined up in piles because she never wanted to put shelves up. Her room wasn't painted beyond the beige walls the apartment came with, but she stopped asking her parents to decorate with her when they let her down for the fourth time, so she did it herself.

Well, she and Noah. Olivia has always been an artist, doodling and sketching from the moment she knew how to hold a pencil. She never liked to show it off, though, not until she was in high school—and even then, she never really had a choice. She was sketching Noah on one of the days they decided they could be around each other in peace, and he caught her looking at him one too many times and figured out she was drawing him. After that, it was a battle of who was stronger, and she was never going to win.

The asshole caught her sketchbook in one hand, his other holding her arms out of the way. There wasn't as much teasing as she imagined, but she didn't speak to him for three weeks regardless. It's not that she thought her artwork was bad—there was just never anyone around to encourage her to show it to others. And she's forever nervous that someone might not like it, as if that should matter to her at all.

Noah was fearless in a way she never could be. He said if he could draw that well he'd shout about it in the streets. But he knew her probably better than anyone else did, so he knew she'd never want that. So, he helped her in the only way he knew how, and the only way she would accept. No, Noah was never artistic, but he would climb on her desk and Blu Tack her artwork to her walls, so she gives him half the credit anyway.

Her bedroom looks mainly the same, but a lot less dusty than she was anticipating. Maybe Helen cleaned it for her to come back to—that is something that Helen would do, because she's the greatest woman to ever exist. Liv wants to go next door for a cup of tea, but it's been so long she doesn't think she'd be able to just walk in now. She'd have to knock, and even that makes her feel like an outsider—and Helen and Joe's home is the only place she ever felt wanted.

Liv knows it's her fault. She barely kept in contact throughout college. She never came back once, and she didn't keep up with messages beyond birthday and holiday cards. At the time, she told herself it was for the best. Now they didn't have to worry about her. But in the four minutes she's been back, looking at the plant she left on the fire escape that's somehow not dead and the way her apartment doesn't smell damp, she realizes it was selfish.

She loves Helen and Joe.

Even if they do have a devil spawn for a son.

CHAPTER THREE

What Olivia really wants is to pass out on her bed, but she thinks she should probably wash the sheets before she does. She's already checked the apartment for major leaks or a loaf of moldy bread, but all she finds is the set of combs she was desperately looking for during the first semester of college. Trying to create clean partings in her hair with a paddle brush so she could do box braids was not her idea of a good time. (Eventually, she found Tanya, who did her hair for her at college and who she misses already. There was never anyone else Black in her apartment building when she was younger, so she struggled to learn through YouTube videos until she convinced Noah to help her.)

Still, she can't be bothered to change her sheets just yet, so she puts it off by unpacking her suitcase, changing into comfy sweats, and texting back her best friend, Steph.

One of the few good things her parents taught her was to not be dependent on anyone. Independence wasn't a trait they instilled in her on purpose; it's just something she picked up on at fourteen years old when she had to cook for herself more often than not. She knows how to rely on herself, and then she can't be hurt. But after three years of living with Steph, Olivia came to understand the idea of codependency. Steph is her best friend in the entire world. They met on the first day of college when they were randomly assigned to be next-door neighbors in a co-ed hall.

They met when Steph went by a different name, but it only took one afternoon of helping each other sort through things they *definitely* could have left at home for Steph to tell Olivia she was transitioning. Olivia was grateful for the information—not because she cared about what gender Steph identified with, as long as she was happy and true to herself, but because it meant Steph trusted her. In forty-five minutes, Steph had seen something in Olivia that meant she had wanted to share it with her.

For the next three years, they spent more time together than they did alone. They put face masks on every Tuesday (Steph had a tutor group on Tuesdays with a passive-aggressive guy who wouldn't stop bullying her until Olivia sent an anonymous tip to the head of department, but by the time the guy got kicked out, the face masks were a tradition). They did laundry together and talked about their fucked-up relationships with their parents, and silently shared a bag of sour sweets under the table at the library whenever they had essays due. They added cringey words and phrases when they were talking for fun and to be ironic, of course. But they used them so much they've actually become part of their vocabulary and now neither of them can type a symbol for an emoji, they have to actually type the words.

It's one of the only relationships Olivia had ever had that she'd fight for if she needed to.

Olivia texts her that she's home, and *yes* she's by herself, and *yes* she will order fries and maybe mozzarella sticks because she's been on the train today *and* unpacked one whole suitcase (even though everything went into the washing bin because she didn't want to pay to wash at college when she was home today—it counts!).

Her phone is already in her hand, so she hovers over the group chat she has with her parents. She's the only one who has messaged in the last three years, but who's counting? Not her!

Liv types out a message and then deletes it. And then she types out another message and deletes it.

On the eighth edit, she sends the text.

Olivia: **Hey, I'm back at home.**

Liv always forgets about the moments after trying to talk to her parents, when dread and excitement work their way up her chest. Will they want to talk, or will they ignore her until they need something? Will they be excited she's home, or will they have forgotten what she looks like? She doesn't need that negativity in her life right now.

So, she puts her playlist on—the one she listens to when she decides she needs a little pick me up (it's mainly girl bands and good for her)—and then she tosses her phone. She aims for the pillow that she threw off the bed when she sat down to text Steph, but it bounces off and hits the floor. It's fine . . . probably.

The sinking feeling kicks in anyway. There's an unwelcome lump in her throat, and she feels foolish for thinking that anything would have changed in the four years since she left, but it's only been about forty seconds since she texted them, so she could calm down. The only thing that ever made her calm down when she felt like she didn't belong anywhere was spending time with Helen and Joe.

And Noah, if she wasn't lying to herself. But she's not in the mood for harsh truths right now.

She wants to go over. She wants to waltz in the door like she used to, without even knocking, because she was always welcome. But she can't go over now because then Helen will ask her where she's been for the past three years. Why hasn't she been home at all? Liv can't tell her why because, firstly, it makes her sound selfish and ungrateful and she's neither of those things, and secondly, she'd never want to upset Helen. Liv truly thinks Helen is made of sunshine and rainbows—hurting her is the last thing she'd ever want to do.

But Liv and Noah spent their entire childhoods together, and she's *still* convinced that if she were on fire, Noah would drink a glass of water instead of saving her. (It's a little dramatic, but she's never denied being so.)

It's not like all kids grow up together and are best friends. She used to gatecrash his birthday parties and she'd be around at Christmas, and when the summer holidays rolled around she spent more time at their place than she did her own. There's a special place deep in her chest that she avoids ever looking at that reminds her of how embarrassed she always was to be the odd one out. To remember how desperately she just wanted to spend an event with her parents, by herself, and she was never able to. She definitely took that away from Noah—and he wasn't old enough to hide his hatred from her.

So it rolled out in passive-aggressive comments about her never wanting to join in on activities and judging them for wanting to play outside. But that was never true—Noah liked Lego and he loved comic books, but he never wanted to share them with her.

Liv was socially awkward from the get-go—something about never being interacted with as a child, according to her therapist—but she's not sure how long she can keep blaming her refusal to talk to new people on her parents.

Her phone buzzes from across the room, and her heart soars in her chest for a moment because Steph's final text said she'd call her later, so if it's not Steph, then one of her parents has finally responded to one of her texts.

Her phone screen lights up when she grabs it from the floor, and she reads that it's a text from "Next Door Annoyance." She groans.

Still, she opens the text from Noah.

Next Door Annoyance: **I hear you're back, dicko**

She replies only because she's polite and she wants to call him out for being a bit fat stalker.

Liv: **Way to be a weirdo—do you have a google alert for me or something?**

"I can hear your empowerment songs from here, Oli," he shouts with his actual voice, which is much worse than through text. He knocks on their shared wall, and she rolls her eyes while groaning "It's *Olivia*." She only makes him call her Olivia because it annoys him and she thinks that's fair for the amount of times he's wound her up before. (Even if hearing his voice properly and not through videos she watched on Instagram sends a sparkle of happiness through her chest, it'll get damped the second he starts talking to her anyway.) Still, she gets up to open her window. Sharing a fire escape with him is honestly the worst thing that ever happened to her.

She leans out the window, obviously. She's not letting him in.

"Hello to you as well, Noah," she drawls. But when she looks over, expecting him to be mirroring her position, he's already sitting cross-legged with his back against the fire escape, looking at her.

"Hi, Oli."

Listen. Noah has always been infuriating, because he can't be anything else, but he's always softened that blow by being unreasonably attractive. The last three years have been kind to him—his smile is bright and his skin darkened in the summer sunshine. He's grown into his ears, and she's pretty sure his shoulders were never that broad, and his arms look a little ridiculous, even if she can't drag her eyes away from them. He also grew out his hair a little (he always used to have it shaved short because he never liked his tight curls). Liv always thought he was cute either way. Not that she'd ever dare tell him that—it's not like he doesn't know he's pretty.

"Mm-hmm," she replies, pulling her bottom lip between her teeth.

Olivia has grown up throughout her time at college too. She hasn't grown any taller, even if Noah appears to have shot up even more, but she's matured. She guesses Noah could have done that as well. He stayed at home for college instead of going further afield. Liv might have done that too—his college has some of the best courses in the country, and she wouldn't have had to get a job at the same time as studying if she lived here—but she was desperate to get out of the apartment she finds herself back in.

"When did you get home?" Noah asks, half leaning into his room. He comes back with a blanket and throws it at her. It's a routine she forgot about—which is obvious when she forgets to catch it and the blanket hits her square in the face.

"Prick," she mutters against the blanket. She can hear Noah laughing, and for a moment, she thinks about throwing it back. But her hand-eye coordination isn't great, and she doesn't feel like walking down four flights of stairs to get his blanket when she throws it over the railing, so she folds it under her arms instead. Noah always sits on the fire escape like he doesn't know it's four floors high and the rickety metal keeping him in place was faulty back when they were in third grade, let alone now. Liv leans against her windowsill, safe, because she's not a Neanderthal.

"Uhm, about two," Liv says.

"Why didn't you call? I would have helped you with your bags," he replies.

"You would have turned up with a sign that says *welcome back from prison.*" She gives him an unimpressed stare as he throws his head back and laughs.

"I can't believe you robbed me of the opportunity, Ols," he says, and she laughs with him. "I would have got you an ice cream as well."

"Oh, it was so busy earlier!" she replies, standing on her tiptoes slightly.

"I know! It's been busy all year, but maybe Marv will let us skip the queue now you're back."

"Oh my God." Liv groans. Marv has asked her out about seventeen times, and she's politely declined every time because he's at least forty-five and she's not interested. But he has the best ice cream on the promenade, so she lets Noah go and buy her ice cream while she sits on the wall and ignores Marv waving at her.

If there's one good thing about Noah—apart from his smile and his jawline—it's his inability to let someone hurt her. Whether that means buying her ice cream from the creepy guy so she doesn't have to see his lingering eyes, or carrying her books home for her in high school when the older girls called her a geek for having so many. (They were mandatory—well, most of them, anyway—so she never really cared what they said, but Noah always glared at the girls as he took her books from her arms, and she let him because they were heavy and her feminism leaves her body the second she starts sweating.)

That doesn't apply to him, though. She remembers how he pushed her into a pool in seventh grade. Arsehole.

"He missed you." Noah laughs, but the smile doesn't reach his eyes. "Perv only gave me one scoop instead of two."

"You only ever pay for one," she says with a laugh.

"Yeah, but he always gives me two if I'm with you! Last year I told him you were back and he gave me a free scoop, and then I had to avoid him for the next week."

"Ah, so that's why you came to say hi . . . You miss the ice cream." Liv rolls her eyes. She leans her chin into her hand, her elbow keeping her upright.

Noah looks at her then, his eyes squinting. She wonders if he's going to tell her he missed her, really and truly. She wonders if she missed him too. Probably, if she allowed herself to think about it. If she ever allowed herself to think about home when she was away, she probably would have found that she did miss him.

But then his face morphs into something she doesn't recognize, and she's not sure if it's because she forgot every iteration of his face recently since she's only seen him through Instagram stories and the very occasional times she let herself look through Helen's feed, or if it's because he's hiding it from her.

Either way, he speaks before she figures it out.

"Exactly. Also, to tell you I washed your sheets so you don't have to do that tonight." He shrugs.

"You did?" Liv asks, her eyebrows high. She doesn't mind that Noah has been in her bedroom—he's been in her bedroom more times than anyone else has. She just forgot he always had her back, even with things that simply don't matter, like wanting to sleep in clean bedding.

"Of course," he replies. "I had an orgy last night, so—"

"You're so—" She laughs, desperately looking for something to throw at him, but she comes up empty handed, so she settles with flipping him off instead. The only thing vaguely throwable is her plant pot with a plant she thought she'd killed before she went away.

"Isn't Larry doing well?" Noah asks, pointing his foot toward the plant she left on the fire escape. They don't need much work—that's the only reason she got that plant in the first place—but they definitely need water at least once in four years.

"Larry?" she asks. She doesn't name her plants because she kills more than she saves, and it feels mean to give them an entire backstory when she's going to be throwing a funeral for them in six to eight weeks.

"Yes. He's my child."

"Hey," Liv says, leaning further than she would like out of her window just so she can shove his thigh with her hand. "That's my child."

"Oh, it is, is it?" He laughs. "I expect four years of child support payments by tomorrow."

"Go away." She laughs back. The silence she was expecting when she entered the apartment rolls over them in a comfortable wave. It's never been awkward with Noah—she just forgot that. She forgot that coming back had some good aspects too.

It's nice, she thinks, being here with Noah. Maybe their relationship will be more than passive-aggressive comments and barging into each other to be the first in the elevator.

CHAPTER FOUR

"**F**iretruck," Noah groans, refusing to move his head from the crook of his elbows as Liv opens the door to his place. (Liv knocked first, but Helen called out that she could come in.)

Firetruck? Really? That's how he wants to start this summer. Prick. She's not even here to see him. Even with the nerves that plagued her overnight about coming back here, she could only last until the next evening to see Helen and Joe.

"I didn't even say anything," she mutters to herself. She can't say it to him because they have this ridiculous agreement that is borderline a non-sexual safe word. They (or she, because he's useless) decided after a decade of winding each other up until they were screaming and crying that they just needed *something* to stop it. Something to say that meant they both had to walk away. And a firetruck happened to drive past that day, with its the lights blaring, as they seethed at each other on their fire escape.

Sometimes neither of them said it and they'd argue long into the night through their bedroom wall. (Noah is the only person in her life she's able to shout at, and he's the only person she'll allow to shout at her—it's the peace they give each other.) Other times, he'd only have to look at her funny for her to shout firetruck, and he'd leave.

Firetruck saved their relationship, and it was barely worth saving.

"Firetruck," Noah repeats.

"Enough bickering, you two." Helen scoffs as she places the bowl of spaghetti in the middle of the table. Liv never liked to cook—it's something she did almost every night before college, and it only reminded her she was always cooking for herself. Helen taught her a few recipes before she went away, and the only reason she kept it up was because when Liv was feeling homesick, it reminded her so much of Helen. Helen taught her how to make a great tomato sauce, and how to get perfectly crispy roast potatoes. She also taught her that sometimes nothing beats grilled cheese.

Olivia often cooked for Steph, who said she's already done one major thing in her life, so she's not learning to cook as well.

But tonight, Liv is excited about Helen's home cooking.

"Hey, sweetheart," Helen says, appearing in front of her while she glares at Noah, who is still lost in a trance.

"Hi," Olivia replies. She wants to reach out and pull her into a hug, even though she's not a hugger at all. It's something they used to playfully tease her about—the way she'd duck and weave whenever Helen or Joe tried to greet her with a hug. The way she'd slam the door in Noah's face if he chased her around the house trying to pick her up because he's a menace to society. But she knew it was always from a place of love. Well, probably not for Noah, he just liked to wind her up, but at least for Helen and Joe.

She didn't realize how much she missed the action while being away. Obviously, she's hugged people—Steph (affectionate) and Brendan (derogatory) and some random girls she met while drunk in the bathroom of a club at college. But Helen is different.

There's not much time to think about it before Helen's pulled her into a hug, her arms tight around her waist. Liv lets her, as she always will, and she tries to breathe through Helen's thick hair that has smothered her face.

"It's so good to see you, sweetie," Helen says, rubbing her back a few times before she pulls back. "Noah has been lost without you."

"Oh, I'm sure," Liv says with a laugh, letting her hands linger against Helen's arms before she fully pulls away.

"I said *firetruck*," Noah repeats, and Liv rolls her eyes because she's not even talking to him anyway.

"Noah, stop," Helen says with a tut. She and Joe put up with a lot of bickering in the past, and Liv is surprised they didn't kick them both out when they turned sixteen. "Ignore him, Livi. Girl drama. Noah, can you get the drinks, please?"

Olivia wonders what the drama is, only because she would have always known before. She knew when he had a crush on Gen in high school, and she knew when he sulked because she barely looked in his direction. She's always known when he liked someone, but now she has no idea. It's what she wanted—the time away, the fresh start. She just never thought she'd miss it so much.

She wants to ask him who the girl is, but she's sure he'll screech "firetruck" in her face for the umpteenth time and she can't be bothered. Besides, she hears the clicking of Joe's office door and feels nervous all over again.

"Did I hear our girl was home?" Joe beams at her as he walks down the hallway. He's always holed up in his office until it hits exactly six p.m. and then he ignores work completely. Sometimes a meeting would overrun, and he would simply leave.

"Hello, trouble," he says, pulling her into a hug.

"Hi, Joe," she mumbles, engulfed by his oversized flannel jacket. He's not a woodworker, but he sure likes to dress like one.

"How was college?"

"Wait, wait," Helen starts, shuffling them all to the table to sit down. "Let's dish and then you can dish."

Liv groans. "There's really not that much to tell," she says, but she humors them anyway. Noah loads her plate with spaghetti and meatballs. It was their tradition—it started in the first few days she was invited over for dinner. She was always too nervous to take a plate full of food first, and then she was too nervous to take very much in case she looked greedy, so Noah started to do it for her. She looks at him to smile in thanks, but he's looking anywhere but at her.

"So," Helen says, "tell us everything . . ."

Everything doesn't take that long, because beyond her best friend Steph, college was just . . . fine. Her classes were fun, and she tells them as much. Helen jokes that she probably picked all the morning classes (true), and Joe asks if she had to do any maintenance herself because that should have been on the landlord (she changed one lightbulb in three years but she doesn't tell him about the mold issues lest he marches there during dinner).

Noah doesn't say anything at all, not really. Olivia asks him how college was, and he says it was great, best experience of his life, but he doesn't elaborate. She wonders if it has anything to do with the girl drama he's having now. She doesn't ask.

She also doesn't tell them about her ex-boyfriend, because in the end, there was really nothing to tell.

"So, what brings you back?" Noah asks. There's something buried in his tone that he's not trying all that hard to hide. She's not sure if he's mad she's back or if he's waiting patiently for her to leave.

"Er, there's a job," she replies, twisting her fork in her hands. His face snaps to hers, something unreadable in his eyes. She guesses both things could be true.

"Here?" Helen asks, her eyes wide. Olivia wishes she never mentioned it, because it was hard enough leaving the first time, and she's not sure she wants this job at all.

"Um, yeah."

"That's exciting!" Joe says, grabbing another slice of bread to mop up the sauce left on his plate. "Noah's missed you. Maybe you could finally finish that puzzle that's taking up space in my office."

"It's still half-complete?" she asks. The puzzle is nothing fancy—it's a watercolor of an English countryside with flowers of all colors. It's her least favorite type of puzzle, the type where you just have to try each piece with another until you find something that fits, as opposed to being able to actively seek out a puzzle piece that has three concave sections and a dot of red. It was one of the only presents she remembers getting from her parents, and it sat unopened in her bedroom for years before Noah said he'd help her with it. Neither of them like puzzles—not really. Noah was always a Lego guy. But he helped her with it every Sunday all the same.

Noah scoffs, tearing a hole in his bread as he tries to butter it with a little too much force. "Well, it's not going to make itself." Liv pretends it's not because he's annoyed at her, because then she'll argue back. After all, he's entirely infuriating, but Helen is at the table, so she keeps her mouth shut.

"I know," she replies, because it's true.

"Alright you two," Joe says with a laugh. "Now you're back, at least for a little while, you can do it or get rid of it and do something else you two like to do so much. Argue in the sun."

Olivia smiles, but she feels guilty. She didn't mean to leave the puzzle incomplete; she just didn't think about it beyond it being something neither of them really wanted to do. She liked to read, and she also liked to sit near people and read, because she's not particularly good at conversations but she doesn't like to be alone.

"Maybe I'll try and read in the sun instead," Liv says with a laugh, then swallows. "I much prefer that."

Noah sighs as he rolls his eyes. "We know. You liked being by yourself and reading books no other six-year-old was reading."

"It's not my fault you couldn't understand the books I was reading," she replies, twisting the food on her plate. She's bored of his passive-aggressive comments. He was completely fine yesterday. "I'm not sure you'd get them now."

"I said *firetruck*," he snaps.

"Oh, for—" She drops her fork. He knows full well that firetruck doesn't count once he's started being an asshole again, but she lets it slide, if only for Helen and Joe.

She'll just have to avoid him for the rest of summer, or until she takes the job hours away and never has to see him again.

CHAPTER FIVE

O livia knew that she needed to go grocery shopping and the kitchen tap leaked. She knew those things the second she walked through the door, but she's only been back for three days, so she wasn't planning on acting on any of that for another six to seven working days. Helen sent her home with leftover spaghetti, so if she ordered takeout over the weekend, she wouldn't need to see the inside of a grocery store until next week.

But Helen and Joe have never cared about her daily plans, not really. So, when it hit eight a.m., they knocked on her door with bags of groceries and a toolbox.

It's familiar. It's still early. But it's mostly nice.

"What are your plans for your birthday, kiddo?" Joe asks, changing the lightbulb in her front room, which Olivia hadn't even noticed was blown.

"Oh . . . I haven't really thought about it."

Olivia doesn't do birthdays. Well, she doesn't do *her* birthday. She loves everyone else's. The past three years have been a collection of brightly colored balloon arches and bunting that remains in her and Steph's living room for three months at a time (because she loves to decorate but hates to take the decorations down because it signals the end of something happy).

Besides, her birthday isn't for weeks.

She always got away with not telling anyone when her birthday was at college by saying it was in the summer holidays, when everyone apart from her had gone home for summer. (Not technically a lie—her birthday is in deep August.) And besides, unless she brings it up, people don't often ask about it.

The only time she ever acknowledged it was her birthday was when she received flowers. Each year she was away, the red carnations turned up at nine a.m. on her birthday. They never came with a card, but they smelled divine and looked pretty in her bedroom, so she never pushed it. Besides, that way she could pretend they were from her parents and another year hadn't slipped past where her dad texts her a week late and her mom's assistant emails her a bookstore gift card in July.

She also got a card from the Grants (Helen, Joe, Noah, and their cat, Murphy), of course.

"Well, you're back now," Joe replies, pulling her into a side hug as he fiddles with his toolbox. He's always itching to fix something, and she lets him, even if she's not sure there's anything else that needs fixing other than the tap, and he already knows he's missing the part to fix that. "So, maybe we could do something."

"Joe," Liv warns. He backs away with his arms up in surrender. She'll prepare herself for a meal and a gift she wouldn't be able to get out of even if she wanted to.

"It won't be as big as Grams's party," Joe promises. "Oh, are you getting those decorations today?"

"I was planning on it, yep," Liv replies.

"Noah will be here soon," Helen says. Liv goes to reply, but Helen gives her a look as she unloads her groceries, stopping it before Liv's whiny reply even makes it halfway up her throat.

"Oh, come on," Olivia mutters, trying to avoid rolling her eyes hard enough to get a headache. It's a little unreasonable, because he is turning up with the bit that Joe needs to fix the tap, which is delightful because Olivia hates the incessant drip that has kept her awake for the past two nights.

But she knows that if Noah turns up now, Helen is going to ask him to help Olivia with getting the decorations for Grandma Grant's annual summer party. Olivia always used to decorate it because she loves to throw a party, but she hasn't been around for the last three parties, so she thought she wouldn't be asked this year. But Helen sent her a text last night asking if she'd like to do it again, something about it "not feeling the same when she was gone," and Olivia jumped at the chance.

She just forgot that Helen always asked Noah to help as well because Helen was convinced that their being together for even more time was the key to fixing their relationship. (She would have helped her anyway, even if she knew Noah would be here, because Helen is her favorite of the Grant family.)

"Be nice," Joe says with a laugh.

"Sorry," Liv mutters. She is nice! (Adjacent.) She hears him coming moments later, the annoying sound of his footsteps thumping through her brain. She hates how she has it memorized. She's tried to purge it from her mind, but with him living next door, stomping around from dawn until dusk with only a thin wall separating their bedrooms, there's nothing she can do.

The door opens a second later, and she groans because she still has bed hair and she's in her pajamas and he's definitely going to mention it.

"Hey," Noah says, his voice kinder than it ever has been with her while he greets Helen. Their family's love language is physical touch and words of affirmation, and somehow Liv loves being around at least two-thirds of them, even though she can't fathom why she'd need to hug someone to say hello.

"Why do you bother knocking if you're going to walk straight in?" Liv asks.

"Are you planning to look like you live in a dumpster all day?" he responds, and Joe slaps his shoulder when he tries to hug him. Liv wants to say something about how he looks, but she turns to give him her unimpressed stare and she's floored, because obviously he looks beautiful.

He always looks beautiful. It's just a fact. The sky is blue, the sun will rise in the morning, and Noah is beautiful. It's a colossal shame about his personality, and the fact he can't be serious for more than three seconds, and that he's *always* around. Sure, she spends a lot of time at his place for events, but before Liv went to college, Noah was always at her place—avoiding his parents, avoiding doing homework, and annoying the living daylights out of her.

"Shut up," Liv grumbles instead. She pulls her pajama top down a little anyway.

"Noah, be nice," Helen chastises.

"I'm always nice," he replies, taking a grape from the bunch Helen had just placed in the fruit bowl.

It reminds Olivia of a simpler time. Nothing much was different—she still woke up alone, and Helen, Joe, and begrudgingly, Noah, came to her aid whether she liked it or not. Now, though, she has to be an adult. She has to navigate life fully on her own. Before, at least she could claim she was a teenager still, so the decision about what she was going to do with the rest of her life wasn't something she had to actively decide upon. It was still three years (nearly four because she took a masters course at the end) of college and partying and having to budget away. But now she's back in the same apartment she was desperate to leave, with the same people who helped get her out—but she has decisions to make, and plans to have, and a life to lead, and it's terrifying.

No less terrifying than getting on the train to come back. But looking at Helen putting food away for her, Joe checking his toolbox for what she thinks is a wrench, and Noah . . . well, smirking at her as he eats her grapes, she thinks with their help, at least, it will be easier to leave.

CHAPTER SIX

Olivia slips on one of her sundresses. It's white and has little strawberries all over it, and she loves it as much as she loves summer. She pulls on some short cycling shorts with it, because she loves summer but will avoid thigh rub like the plague.

She twists half of her hair up into a bun and lets the other half flow in curls behind her back. She misses her braids, but no one at home can do them as well as Tanya at college can, so she cut her losses and took them out before she came back. She sprays sun cream over her exposed skin, and she follows it with bug spray behind her knees and near her elbows because she's a mosquito magnet and she's not about to spend the entirety of summer covered in red bumps.

She packs her bag for summer, which is always just an oversized beach bag even if she's not going to the beach. It's always full of the same stuff—sun lotion, her reusable cup, and hand sanitizer (because she will get ice cream and it will drip down her fingers and she refuses to have sticky hands for longer than three seconds), a separate tote bag in case she finds a cute plant pot, her purse, keys, and five tubes of lip balm (lest one of them dries up, she manages to lose one down a drain, or a seagull steals four. She refuses to ever have dry lips).

When she's done getting dressed, she can't hear anything, so she knows Helen and Joe have left. She bites back a groan at having to spend the day with Noah, because he is simply incapable of not talking. He loves the sound of his own voice and uses it to drivel on about absolutely nothing. Or, even worse, he'll ask her questions about things he missed for the last four years (not that he was all the bothered at dinner last night, so maybe she'll get away with reading on her phone when they stop for a drink) and there's something about his face that makes it difficult for her to lie to him, but she doesn't want to spend the day explaining the horrors that run free in her mind.

So, she makes a quick mental list of topics they can talk about if he insists on spending the day talking. Otherwise, he runs out of things to say, and somehow, they always end up arguing when he really could just be quiet.

"Ready," she calls, walking to the front door to slip her sandals on. When she looks over, he's sitting on the couch looking entirely too at home. She doesn't mind him being comfortable—she likes it when people are comfortable enough to be themselves—but she doesn't like him being in the front room with his shoes still on. What an animal.

"Alright," he replies, sighing as he gets off the couch like he's had such a tiring day being annoying and doing nothing at all (apart from going to the store to get the part they needed to quickly fix her tap, but whatever). He's in no semblance of a hurry, and she swears she can hear him smirking, but she won't give him the satisfaction of looking at him. God, he's infuriating. She's not sure how she's going to last the day.

"We're only like six blocks away," she says, refusing to give Noah all the bags when he asks. They're not heavy, and she knows he just wants to hold them to make it more difficult for her to walk to get strawberries.

"It's in the wrong direction, Lils," he replies, his eyes on some black-and-white bunting.

Olivia has already settled on a bright color theme for the party. Every year there is a different theme. Grams loves old movies, so they did black-and-white for her seventy-third birthday four years ago. She's seen photos of the past three years, so she knows bright colors haven't been an option.

She's explained that to Noah in the first three shops they've been into.

"It won't even take that long." She sighs. She wants the strawberries so badly. She could just go tomorrow.

"I'm not going six blocks to buy something you can buy next door."

The reason Olivia hates to ask for things is because the person you're asking might say no. Steph always says "the worst they can say is no," as if that's not entirely devastating. As if Olivia doesn't think about the "no" for the next seventeen working days.

Luckily, she doesn't care enough about Noah for him to count. He drew on her favorite book when they were younger, so really, he should go with her to get strawberries. (He did say it was an accident, and he did replace it a few weeks later, but still. Strawberries.)

"Noaaaah . . . Come on, after all the hard work getting the decorations, we deserve—"

"You weren't even here for the last three, Oli," he mutters, entirely interrupting her. She lets him get away with it because she's embarrassed she's been called out for it. She's surprised that he sounds mad about it—as if they ever did anything apart from bicker the entire time.

"I was at college," she replies, but the excuse feels feeble, even as it leaves her tongue.

Noah scoffs at her, but he puts the bunting down all the same.

"I was," she repeats.

"I know."

"So why are you mad?" she asks. She wasn't going to bring it up last night, so she let him get away with being a dick over dinner, but she's hungry and too hot in this store and her shoulder hurts from carrying her bags around even though she could simply hand them to Noah but she won't.

"It doesn't matter." He huffs, then moves away. He's turned the corner and is walking down another aisle before she registers that he's gone.

When she had to leave for college, Noah practically shoved her out the door, her suitcases in his hands. He was all but running to the car and throwing her bags into the boot. He took the drive with her and his parents, but she knows Helen forced him to go. He also spoke about how he'd get a decent night's sleep now that she wasn't snoring next door (she doesn't snore; she recorded herself sleeping just to check) and how he was going to sit on their shared fire escape and not worry about her coming to annoy him every three seconds.

So she's not sure why he's got a stick up his ass now.

She follows him to the next aisle ready for a fight, but she realizes midway that she doesn't have a defense. She wasn't there for the past three years. He's not wrong. She just doesn't know why he's being a bit of a prick about it. But he's always a bit of a prick, so whatever.

Her stride doesn't keep up with her mind, and she's barreled down the aisle, brows furrowed, before she can stop herself.

"That's cute," she spits out when she doesn't know what to say, her eyes on the notebook Noah is turning over in his hands. "Notebooks with initials are cute."

"Dammit."

"What?" she asks, her brows furrowing again as he puts the notebook down. Surely he wasn't planning on buying it for her anyway.

"Nothing," he says with a sigh.

"Right. Of course. You know you could have stayed at home if you were going to be difficult all day?" she says, her brows high as he looks at her. She widens her eyes when he doesn't relent.

"I . . ." His eyes flick over her face. She watches him figure out if he wants to tell her the truth. He doesn't, but she takes it anyway. "There's a girl."

"*Ohhhh.*"

"But she's nothing like you, so she won't like the notebook," he says with a huff, shoving his hands in his pockets.

"Does she even like notebooks at all?" Olivia asks, and Noah chews on his bottom lip. She's unsure why some guys seem to think all girls are made in cookie-cutter shapes, as if they could pick anything from a generic list and it would fit one out of three girls.

"Er, good question." He laughs, though there's no humor behind it. He runs his hand through his hair, and Olivia has to blink a couple of times to get the image out of her head.

"Come on," she says, handing him one of the bags as an olive branch. "Let's go get a drink and I'll help you figure out what she wants."

"You'll help me?"

"Even though you're the most annoying person I know? Sure."

As luck would have it, Noah turns out to be not the most annoying person she's been around today. That title stays with the elderly woman who stopped in front of her seven times (yes, *seven times*, she counted!) at the party store while she was trying to pick napkins that matched the theme for Grandma Grant's party.

He's still the worst person she's ever met, but he does appear to have done some growing up in the time she's been away. She won't tell him that, though. Liv spent the day wondering if he thought she had changed—if he thought she was more mature than before, like she did with him, or if he thought she was funnier than he remembered.

Though she doesn't care what Noah thinks right now because they finally found a café that didn't have a line outside (she loves to be by the seaside, but apparently so does everyone else, and she can barely see the front of the shops through sun hats and folded-up deck chairs) and she can smell the pastries from the bathroom as she washes her hands. She's excited to see which summer-themed drink she's going to try. They're usually pink and full of enough sugar to make her worried her teeth are going to melt, but she's a sucker for them anyway.

So she's slightly disappointed when she comes out of the bathroom and Noah is already sitting at the corner booth, their bags propped between him and the window, and he has two drinks in front of him.

"Did you order for me?" Liv asks when she gets to the table.

"Mm-hmm," he replies, tapping away at something on his phone.

"Oh. Thanks," she replies. It's a little frustrating because she wanted to order some food as well, but it would be awkward to go up now, so she sits down with a slightly forced smile. He did use her reusable cup, so she can't be too mad.

She takes a sip, and . . . *oh*.

"Strawberry?" she asks, going back for another sip as the bubbles burst along her tongue.

"Yeah. You love to try the summer flavors," he casually replies. He places his phone down on the table with a small thump. She wonders if he's still frustrated about *the girl* like he seemed to be while looking at notebooks. She figures now is as good a time as any to help him out.

"What?" she asks, her straw between her teeth.

"Are you dating anyone?" he asks a little awkwardly, if she had to guess the emotion. It's not wildly out of the blue, because they used to tell each other everything, if only to keep the other's parents off their backs. Well, mainly Helen and Joe, because Liv could have been having all-nighter parties at sixteen and her parents would be none the wiser.

"Er . . ." She laughs and looks at the table. It's not like it's a difficult question, but she feels like he's put her on the spot. Her nose scrunches without her say-so.

"No."

Olivia tried dating in college—honestly and truly, she did—but there's something about her personality that people don't like. One guy told her she was too cool for him, and not in a good way. Not in a "she knows everything about sports, how hot" kind of way (which really just means he wants her to wear a sports jersey and cheer for the same team as him), but in a "she knows more about things he'll never understand" kind of way (which means he's not interested in her enough to make any effort at all, which is rude and offensive because she never asked him to be).

She wasn't always unsuccessful. She'd dated Brendan for six months and ended up heartbroken at the end because he was transphobic to her best friend. She didn't love him or anything, but she liked him a lot, and despite her track record of important people in her life letting her down, she was still momentarily surprised she'd got it so wrong.

"Here you are."

The words make Olivia jump because they didn't come out of Noah's mouth, and a little of her drink spills onto the table. Noah wipes it up with a napkin before she's even registered because her eyes are trained on the plate of miniature pastries being placed in front of her.

"Oh, thank you."

"God, I was starving," Noah says, loading one of the side plates with a croissant, a sausage roll, and the only cinnamon roll. Dammit.

He slides the plate over to her, taking the empty one for himself. It's not clear for very long, the piles of savory and sweet treats stacking up a little too close together for her liking.

"Try this," he urges, passing her part of his jam croissant.

"Thanks," she says, weary. She swipes her finger through the pile of jam and wipes in on the side of her place. Though, she has to lick her finger either way because she doesn't like the stickiness jam leaves behind.

"You're a savage," he says with a laugh. He takes a bite. Olivia thinks it's apricot. "I can't believe you'd rather have a plain croissant and not one with jam."

"Hmm. My dad always bought me these when we went out at the weekend, and that's always what he had. They're nice," she says with a smile.

Noah's face drops, but she's just shoved the last half of the pastry into her mouth, so she can't ask him what's wrong right now.

"What?" she asks once she's swallowed, because his eyebrows still haven't settled back into their neutral position. She takes another sip of her strawberry lemonade while he blinks a couple of times. It might be her favorite drink this summer already.

"Nothing."

She gives him a look but doesn't push it further. If he doesn't want to tell her, that's his right. She's not entirely sure she cares either way.

Noah avoids her gaze as she eats the cinnamon roll then licks the crumbs from her fingertips as she tries to remember what topics of conversation she thought up earlier.

She flicks through the thoughts in her head. She could ask how his last year at college went, but then she'd have to ask about years one through three as well, because beyond the odd message about the post, she doesn't know what he's been up to at all. She could ask him what his plans are for this summer, but she thinks that'll make it seem like she wants to know so she can slide into his plans like she did for nearly nineteen years.

It should be awkward, the silence that's swept over them, but it's not. Not really.

She wishes she had her sketchbook with her, because Noah has his straw behind his ear and the sleeves of his top are rolled up ever so slightly and he has a light sunburn on his nose. He gets it every year because he refuses to reapply sunscreen, and despite his brown skin, he gets a sun-kissed glow.

She likes to draw him. He's nice to draw. She wonders if anyone else has drawn him since she's been gone. If he's had a girlfriend, and if he has new friends beyond Aaron, Matty, and Dave from high school. It's a strange thought that she shoves to the back of her mind because she's not sure why she'd care about that either way.

"So," she says. "Who's the girl?"

CHAPTER SEVEN

One of the benefits of living in a tourist town is that the shops stay open late into the evening. It's almost dark when they leave the coffee shop with a bag full of pastries they couldn't eat.

"I have no idea what to get Mom for her birthday this year," Noah grumbles, running the back of his hand over his forehead. They spent at least an hour in the coffee shop, and despite her questions about the girl drama, all she got from it was that her name is Beth and she has a new boyfriend. She's not even sure Beth and Noah ever went on an actual date—he was far too cagey about the information.

Olivia tried to give him some advice either way, drawing on some of her relationships at college and why they failed. She only had one relationship that she'd say actually went anywhere, but she also had a handful of dates that were beyond useless. Noah asked what happened, and she tells him that mainly it was a "her" issue. She wasn't present enough, or she didn't seem interested enough. He laughs when she tells him Brendan hated her film commentary.

Apparently, he's over talking about it now.

"I got her the 'Can't Help Falling in Love' record," Liv replies. "Maybe you could get her your parents' first dance song?"

"Huh?"

"Your dad just got his old record player working again—he mentioned it at dinner—and your mom was talking about how they don't have their wedding songs on record yet. I double-checked earlier," she says, dodging a fast walker on the pavement. The movement bumps her into Noah. She feels him push her back a little. Rude.

The idea had come to her years before, if she's honest. She'd spent the summer between school and college fixing her mother's record player because her mom used to talk about how songs sound better on vinyl. She saved money from her weekend job to buy the record from their wedding day. Liv hadn't been there—she wasn't even born when they got married—but she thought it might bring back nice memories of days when they could all dare to be in the same room as each other.

It didn't matter, obviously. The gift remained unopened when she left for college, and she's pretty sure if she looked in her parents' room, the record player would still be there, unused.

"Seems a bit weird," Noah replies, his brows furrowed as he looks ahead.

Rude, as always, but Liv does want Helen to have something she likes, so she says, "Okay . . . What about—"

"I didn't actually ask for your help," Noah snaps, moving to the side of the pavement so he can stop.

"What's your problem?!" she asks, pushing her hand through her hair.

"Nothing!" he says, his voice strained. She knows he knows he's out of order, she's just not sure why. She's not sure she cares, either.

"You've been snippy all evening, Noah. First, you ask for help about your girl issues—"

"You offered," he replies. And it's true, but she didn't really have any other choice.

"You know you didn't have to come with me?" she says instead.

"Wow. I forgot that I could do anything at all without you."

Liv feels her face drop, the back of her throat burning with embarrassment that everything she thought about their relationship has been true. He's barely tolerated her. She pulls it back, but she knows it's too late. He's already seen it. She speaks before he has the chance.

"Well, I'm telling you that you can. I can carry these home myself."

He scoffs. "Fine."

Liv rolls her eyes at him as she immediately turns to storm down the street. God, he's so annoying. He doesn't follow after her. Good. She doesn't want to walk home with him anyway. She likes her own company.

Sure, it would have been in her better interest to have started walking in the right direction. And sure, it's a little darker than she would like, especially considering she now has to walk to the end of this unreasonably long road before she can turn around and come back, lest someone looks at her from their apartment and watches her turn around in the street for no reason. She figures she could pretend she forgot something, though she's not sure what when she's got six bags in her hands.

She's not panicked, because she knows this town. She's always lived in this town. So she's not worried about walking home while the sky turns from pink to dusky blue.

Besides, it's not like she's not been left alone before. It's all she knows.

"Lils!"

"It's Olivia, Noah," she replies.

"Come on," he says, reaching for her wrist to stop her before they walk entirely in the wrong direction. "Please stop walking. I'm sorry—I didn't mean that."

"Yeah, you did. At least own it, Noah. You don't like me. You don't have to pretend you do."

The words hurt on her tongue, even though she's known it's true for as long as she can remember. She's not sure she ever actually disliked Noah. Sure, he frustrated her, and she remembers screaming "firetruck" in his face more times than she can remember saying something nice to him, but she still leaned on him—like when she didn't know what was wrong one Sunday morning, so she crawled through his window at eight a.m. just to sit in silence and read her book. (She'd figure out later that the unsettled feeling in her stomach was loneliness, not an aversion to gluten like she'd thought. She has that, too, but she still eats garlic bread like it's going out of fashion.)

"It's not—I don't dislike you, Ol. I've never disliked you."

"Don't lie to me," she says with a sigh. He's probably the only person in the world she trusts to tell her everything, even if it would hurt her. She's not ready to lose that just yet.

"We're not kids anymore. Besides, I've never lied to you." He runs a hand through his hair. "I've just had a frustrating morning on top of a bad week."

"That means nothing to me, Noah. Your girlfriend's problems don't mean you can—"

"I know, I know," he says, interrupting her, but she lets him get away with it, barely. "I don't need to take my frustrations out on you. I just—she's not my girlfriend, and I—I'm waiting to find out if I got into the residency program at the Children's Hospital."

"What?" she asks, shocked. She always knew Noah was great with kids. She always knew he was kind, and that he wanted to help whenever he could. He's always been the smartest person she knows, so him wanting to be a doctor shouldn't shock her at all.

She just didn't realize she had missed so much. She had always known everything about him, whether she wanted to or not—but it turns out leaving for three years means she missed a lot. There's a thought niggling at the base of her skull that likes the fact he'll still be here. The Children's Hospital is right around the corner. If she ever wanted to come back home, Noah would be right here.

"I just—I *really* want to get in, and I haven't heard back yet, and I'm so stressed out."

She can feel the fury leaving her in waves. She can practically see the red tendrils of anger floating away until all that's left in her view is Noah. Doctor Grant. And she wants the worried lines between his eyebrows to soften. If only because she doesn't have her sketchbook right now, and Noah's frustrated face is one of her favorite masterpieces.

"Well, I'm sure you got in, Noah. You were always great with kids, and you studied so hard in high school. You know . . ." she says, tapping his foot with her sandal. "When you weren't flirting with Genevieve Jasper."

"Oh, shh," he says, but he laughs.

"When did you send the application in?"

He looks down at the ground, though she can see the upturn of his lips as he does.

"Yesterday."

"Noah," she groans, her face unimpressed as he looks upward, still not meeting her gaze. "They take weeks to look at applications!"

"I know!"

"You're ridiculous," she says with a laugh, but her heart isn't quite in it.

"I know." He sighs. "I'm sorry for being a prick. Can I still walk you home?"

"I'm not happy about it," she mumbles, letting him turn her around as he takes the bags from her.

"I'd expect nothing less."

CHAPTER EIGHT

O livia allows herself a couple of days in the apartment to wallow in her self-pity. It's something she lets herself do a few times a year. She's been back at home for a week—seven whole days—and her parents have said nothing. They haven't even texted her back, let alone turned up at the house.

She shouldn't be surprised. It's nothing original. The same embarrassment and heartache from her teen years. From her childhood, if she's honest, but she was a little too young to understand. Maybe she thought that if she'd changed over the last three years, maybe they had too.

Alas, she's the one checking her phone every three minutes to see if they're typing, or if they've even looked at their phone since she sent the message. Maybe they have new numbers and didn't think she was important enough to know about them.

Oh well. She has the leftover pastries from the shopping trip with Noah. The decorations aren't needed for a few more days, and she's successfully replied to seven out of ten of Steph's rants. So, really, she's thriving . . . Just as someone who likes to lie in bed and only get up one time in three days to shower. (She felt bad about it, but then she showered this morning before throwing herself in clean pajamas and back into bed, so she's not as bothered now.)

Really, she wants to allow herself a whole week to wallow, but Noah is the most frustrating guy alive, so by day three, he's hitching the corner of her window up and letting himself in her bedroom.(Her window is always unlocked because Noah used to sneak when he missed curfew and she got bored of having to get out of bed to unlock four latches when he didn't get the hint that she was pretending to be asleep.)

"You have a key." She groans and throws the pillow over her face.

"Like you don't have something barricaded against the door," he says with a sigh, and she can hear his eyes rolling from here.

"Take the hint, then."

"Get up."

"Noah," she warns. She can hear him getting closer to the bed, and she sends her leg out to kick him, but he grabs her ankle.

"Oli, get up," he replies, dragging her closer to the end of the bed.

"How do you think I can get up when you're manhandling me?" She grunts, then throws the pillow at him. It hits him in the face, and she smiles.

"I can smell you from my bedroom. This is a public health hazard. I'm saving the apartment building and—"

"I showered this morning!"

"Well," he says, pouting a little as he clearly attempts to think of another lie. "Get up anyway. I'll get you some pancakes."

That has her pausing to consider. "Promise?" she asks, squinting at him. He drops her leg to the ground with a thump.

"I've never lied to you."

"You just told me you could smell me from your bedroom," she says as she sits up.

"A teeny tiny fib. That's not the same thing. Besides, you're up!"

She looks at his smile and sighs. "You are, without a doubt, the most annoying person in my life."

Noah does, in fact, get her pancakes. She gets Nutella and banana on hers, and Noah gets bacon and maple syrup. She gives him half of hers.

It's nice to be outside, which is annoying because she always sees those motivational messages plastered to the side of buses or on Instagram ads that say sunshine and movement are some of the best medicine if you're feeling down, and she hates it because it's the last thing she ever wants to do when her brain feels like a storm cloud. She feels herself lifting her face to the sun anyway, and really, she's just a houseplant with complicated emotions.

If Noah hadn't checked something on his phone he refuses to tell her about and wasn't now sulking, she would say she was having a nice day. Liv tried to tell him that the hospital would send his acceptance through the post, but she's not sure that's why he's upset.

She doesn't care, either.

They walk past the promenade, the bright sun partially hidden behind the bridge. Noah grumbles beside her as he kicks stones out of his path, and it forces a memory into Olivia's mind.

They're eleven years old, she has ice cream melting down her fingertips, and she's just finished licking the last of it from the cone. She never liked to eat the wafer, if she could help it—it was always a little too wet and not at all as crunchy as she thought it should be.

She didn't have a bag with her because it was a last-minute outing for her birthday. At the time, she didn't know the Grants had taken her to the arcade and for ice cream because she had no other plans for her birthday—she figured that out a few years later. But it never mattered. It still was and always would be one of the best days of her life.

She won three toys in the penny slot machines that day (she still has them in her room—they're part of the handful of things she took to and from college with her), then she had a chocolate and hazelnut ice cream that ran down her hands until Noah gave her a tissue from his backpack. They'd spent the afternoon bickering, as per their relationship, the word "firetruck" being tossed around like confetti, but he never left her side, either.

Olivia smiles now as she looks at the sunset, and at the same guy annoying the living daylights out of her. The only thing she's missing is ice cream. She wants to suggest they get one because it'll cheer Noah up and she prefers him when he's happy, but then she'll have to be the one to go over, and she can't see who's behind the counter, but she doesn't have the will in her today to tell Marv she doesn't want to date him. Again.

"Do you remember my eleventh birthday?" she asks, swinging her hands lightly next to her. The sun is shining down on the top of her head, and she tilts her face slightly with her eyes closed because she likes when the back of her eyelids turn orange. Noah holds her arm gently as he moves her out of the way.

"Thanks," she mutters.

"Mm-hmm. I do remember winning four toys compared to your three at the arcades, yes," he replies, and she can hear the smile in his voice.

"You had more coins than me!" She pouts, then eases her eyes open and catches Noah smiling at the ground.

"I gave you half of mine. Don't be a sore loser."

"Anyway . . ." she says dismissively. "Maybe I'll do that for my birthday this year."

"Woah!" Noah gasps, his hand against his chest. "Not you having birthday plans!"

"Oh, shut up," she replies, rolling her eyes. "You're not invited."

"Mm-hmm." He laughs. "Hey, you wanna get an ice cream?" Noah asks, pulling his wallet out of his back pocket.

"Yes," she replies, practically skipping after him. "Can I—"

"Oli, you haven't changed your ice cream order since we were kids. Are you saying college changed you that much?"

"It's *Olivia*, and shh," she replies. She lets him go and leans against the brick wall to wait for him. They used to sit here whenever they came out to the promenade. It was their spot, even if she only ever thought it in her head. If they had to meet up, it would always be here. She can't get up onto the wall anymore. Not because she's old and decrepit—well, not really. More she's not about to scuff up her knees by scrambling onto the wall, and she's not tall enough to jump up. But she used to love sitting up here, watching the ferryboats go past.

"Guess how many scoops I paid for," Noah says cheerfully. Olivia looks at the cone in one hand and the pot in the other. Four scoops in total. Then she looks back at the shop and sees Marv eyeballing her.

"Two."

"Ah, the 'Olivia is pretty and Marv is gross' system working for me once again." He smiles.

"Shut up," she says with a groan, but she takes her pot of ice cream from him with thanks.

"Hold this for a sec, please," he asks, handing her his ice cream. She tries a bit before he can tell her not to. Noah never gets the same flavor twice. Today's is banana and toffee. It's pretty good.

His hands drop to her waist, and he lifts her up, placing her on the wall. She yelps but hides it behind her ice cream—but with the way Noah barks out a laugh, she doesn't think she hid it very well.

"Don't say anything," she says, her heart in her chest as Noah jumps with ease to sit next to her.

"Wouldn't dream of it."

It's quiet as they eat, both kicking their feet continuously because it's the only way to stop seagulls swooping in for their ice creams. Occasionally, Noah will wave his hand in the air, and Olivia knows he just prevented her being attacked from behind. The sun is hot against her back, and it warms her through to her core. Summer in college was nice. The trees still turned deep green, and Liv and Steph had some pot plants—that Steph managed to keep alive—on their windowsill.

But it was nothing compared to this. The waves crashing on the seawall below them. The chirps of the birds, and the squeal of tourists that haven't learned how to deal with them yet. She watches a family playing catch on the grass, a child no older than three, if she had to guess, trying and failing to catch the ball in either of their hands. She smiles against her ice cream.

Summers at college also didn't have Noah, which was a good thing—is a good thing—but she doesn't mind him being here now.

"Are you going to invite Steph up for your birthday?" Noah asks, taking a bite out of his cone. He's such a fast eater, but maybe he doesn't need to reminisce over lost summers because he was here the whole time.

"Um, well, I'll invite her up at some point." She shrugs.

He laughs. "She doesn't know when your birthday is, does she?" It's not mean. He's never mean.

"Nope," Liv replies with a pop of her lips. She digs her spoon into the chocolate-hazelnut ice cream, and it tastes like her childhood.

"Well, I guess you're gonna have to let me come with you, then, unless you're going to be the weirdo in the arcade all by yourself."

"Will you let me win?" she asks, scooping some ice cream onto her spoon and handing it to him. He always gets her two scoops, and she only ever eats half. He eats it from her hand instead of grabbing the spoon because he's ridiculous, but she laughs all the same.

"I'll think about it."

CHAPTER NINE

"It's not the worst, but I don't love it." Steph sighs over the phone. She sounds tired, and it has nothing to do with the fact it's eight a.m. and she's on FaceTime with Olivia as she paints her toenails.

Steph left college a couple of days before Olivia, but she's still only been home for about a week. Olivia thought she'd have longer before Steph wanted out. Liv knew Steph's home life wasn't everything she ever wanted, but she hoped she'd have a little longer before shit hit the fan.

"Wanna talk about it, wanna vent, or shall I distract you?"

Steph isn't wearing her hair down and is wearing an outrageously baggy top, which Liv could chalk up to the fact it's barely morning, but she's not sure she's ever seen Steph without something pink on. Right now, she doesn't look like herself at all. The fact she has to hide herself at home, where she should be the safest, makes Liv feel sick. She wants to turn up and scream at Steph's parents and wrap her in a blanket and bring her home with her.

But she can't do that, because Steph is still trying to mend her relationship with her parents, and it's not Liv's place to get involved. So, she does what she can.

"Distract me," Steph replies, her tongue between her teeth as she swipes the nail polish over her toes.

"Mkay, let's do the personality quiz we tried to start during finals."

"Oh! I can't wait to be read to filth and then be depressed about it while changing nothing," Steph says, sitting up cross-legged on her bed.

"Ha! Same. Okay, the Enneagram test," Olivia starts, leaning against her headboard. "Sheesh. It has one hundred and five questions, but then they give us a personality type from one to nine. Here, let me send you the link and we can do it for each other."

"It says people usually focus on the good parts of their personality, but we should also look at the things we could improve." Steph scoffs. "As if I need improving."

Liv laughs. "Alright. It's only for a laugh anyway. So, accurate or inaccurate . . ."

"You know, they don't know what the fuck they're talking about anyway," Steph says, pacing around her room. Her results didn't call her out that bad. They said she was a type three, which just means she's confident and sure of herself (which she is). But Steph says it sounds like she's a bitch (which she isn't). It might be something to do with being called an "overachiever—because the more awards and accolades they have, the more they believe there's something to love about them."

Steph was in every extracurricular she could get into at school, desperately trying to impress her parents with achievements that stretched beyond her gender. Maybe doing the personality test was a mistake.

"It's alright to want to prove yourself, Steph," Liv replies. "It's alright to want to be more than your gender."

"Says you," Steph says with a laugh, then says, "Type nines are just cute."

"I always am," Liv replies, rolling her eyes sweetly. Her result didn't call her out in any way she wasn't expecting. It says she fears being needy and will push people away instead. She's not sure she ever actively pushed her parents away, but she certainly didn't force them to stay.

"My parents are calling," Steph says with an eye roll. "Call you later?"

"Mm-hmm. Oh, what are you doing next week?" Olivia asks, ruminating over her personality type.

"Never leaving my room, watching Desperate House-wives—"

"We just did a marathon!"

"Shh!" Steph laughs. "I suppose I should be looking for a job as well. Lame. I do think I'm just gonna work at a café or something until I figure out what I wanna do—something that gets me out of the house."

"Well, as important as that all is," Liv replies, trying to keep her tone as lively as Steph's, even if it's a joke. "Fancy a trip to the seaside?"

Steph gasps, her smile wide before she's even answered. Olivia watches her face morph from happiness to annoyance as her bedroom door swings open.

"I'm booking tickets right now, bye."

Olivia's phone screen turns back to her background, a photo of the promenade at sunset, and she laughs at the way Steph always hangs up on her. There's no grand goodbye—it takes her half a second at best. Sometimes she throws her a wave, but mostly she has to do something else, so she just does.

If Olivia needs to hang up or leave somewhere, she spends a good twenty minutes working up to actually saying she has to leave. It takes a solid six iterations of "Well, this has been fun" and slapping her hand on her thigh with a sigh to actively get up and leave.

Olivia wishes she was a type-three personality. The dominating, take-no-shit type. The girl that can say no and it's a full sentence. She admires their confidence, and the way they don't let people walk all over them. Every night in bed, she lays her head against the pillow and thinks about how she could have called out the guy on the street that barged into her, or how she would have got the internship she wanted if she'd stood up for herself more.

But she's such a type nine it hurts. Sure, she'll help, and no, the offensive remark about her hair in the middle of class didn't upset her at all! She spends her time in the shower overthinking arguments, while in the moment she says nothing at all, relying on vague dirty looks.

She cries when she's mad, and very rarely when she's actually sad because nothing is ever that sad anymore.

And she's never been comfortable enough around anyone to say she doesn't want to do something.

She's never learned to say no.

CHAPTER TEN

"N o."

"Oh, Oli, come on."

"You know that's pathetic, right?" she says, putting the can of peaches down.

"Yes," Noah responds as he picks it back up, placing it in the basket. "But I don't care what you think about me, so I can ask you with my pride still intact."

"Are we sure you have any pride at all?"

"Oli," he whines, his head tilted back. "I've just seen her here with a new guy, and it's barely been two weeks."

"I'm not pretending to be your girlfriend. I can barely stand to be around you at the best of times," she says, eyeing a jar of jam. She already has a jar in the fridge, but it's not her favorite, so she's considering buying a black cherry jam as well.

"I'm your favorite person in the universe, Liv! Be a better liar." He says it like he truly believes it. Like he didn't have the same childhood as her—as if everything she thinks about their relationship is wrong. He's useless.

Noah is also useless to shop with. He never adds anything to the list when they're at home, and he just stands near her at the grocery store and carries the basket. So, sort of helpful, because she does want to get a bag of ice and some fizzy drinks.

That's enough sugar, she thinks, so she puts the jam back.

"You're deluded," she responds.

"You're so mean to me, and for what?" he says with a laugh. He takes the jam from the shelf and puts it into the basket. Liv rolls her eyes, but at least she can have jam on toast for dinner.

"It's only ever deserved, Noah. We just need ice and Coke now. I'll grab the Coke and you get the ice, and I'll meet you by the checkout?"

"Mkay, loser pays!" he says, all but running away. He's the only loser, but she smiles either way. He will definitely be the one to pay as well, because she was already next to the drinks aisle, and she can see an open conveyor belt.

But even after she's waited a few minutes, Noah is nowhere to be seen. She sighs, wondering what he's looking at, what random item he wants to buy. She sets off to look, wishing she'd only picked up one bottle and not a large pack of cans. She just thinks drinks taste better in cans.

She hears it before she sees it. Noah is uncomfortable. She doesn't like it—the way he switches from foot to foot, and the way he laughs like his vocal cords are being wrung out.

The thing about Noah and Liv is that they have each other's backs, no matter what. And she knows if she became deluded enough to want to fake date him to make another guy jealous (she thinks—she's still not sure what the point behind it is, but she doesn't have to understand it to help him out), he would do it for her. And listen, she's not possessive, and Noah isn't hers and she would never want him to be, but still, she waltzes over.

"Baby," she starts, attempting not to grimace because she's thought about pet names before, just pillow thoughts, and "baby" was never one of them but it just slipped out. "Hi. Hi, baby . . . uhm, do you want to get chicken for tonight?"

"Baby?" the lady in front of him asks with a tone Olivia doesn't enjoy but she's sure is warranted. The woman (Liv assumes she's Beth, because otherwise why would she be draping herself in front of the guy she's with all dramatically if she's not the one Noah was talking about?) flicks her eyes between Noah and Liv like she's not quite sure how that happened. Rude. Noah's not that bad.

"Chicken sounds great," Noah replies, looking directly at Liv with a smile. He wraps his arm around her shoulder, pulling her closer. "Thanks."

Someone clears their throat, and thank goodness, because Noah was looking at her a little too long and he's a much better actor than she is. If she didn't know any better, she'd think he actually liked her.

"Oh, sorry." He laughs. "Oli, this is Beth. Beth, this is Olivia."

"Does she always have two names?" Beth asks, with her perfectly shaped eyebrow (Liv's jealous—her brows are pretty good too, but she has to work for it) arched toward her hairline, her hair flowing in blonde locks behind her.

"I just have one," Olivia replies, rolling her eyes. She doesn't like to point out when people are being rude, as being confrontational is not something she enjoys, but being talked about while she's standing right there is one of her pet peeves. Her parents used to do it all the time. She hated it then, and she hates it now.

"Only I'm allowed to call her Oli. Boyfriend privileges," Noah replies, his hand squeezing Liv's waist.

"You are not," she replies, playfully elbowing him in the side.

"Oli," he groans, his hand slipping to her waist to pull her closer. He presses his lips against her hairline, and she thinks *Calm the fuck down.*

"Firetruck," she whispers between gritted teeth. She's not a PDA girl, even if it is fake.

Noah pulls back, his eyes tracking her face like he's done something awful. As if they don't use firetruck when the other moves the salt just out of reach on the dinner table. She rolls her eyes, rubbing her thumb over his back.

"Right." Beth sighs. "Are you coming to Aaron's party tonight?"

Olivia isn't sure she's invited, even though she used to know Aaron at high school. Something in the way Beth only looks at Noah, something in her tone, something in the way she purses her lips says probably not.

"We'll be there," Noah says triumphantly. It's a little rude of him to answer for her; she might have plans. (She doesn't, and she's eighty percent sure Noah knows that from the carton of ice cream she put in the basket, but still, does it hurt to *ask?*)

"It'll be good to see you both there," Beth's boyfriend says to Olivia. If she had to guess by the way he smiles at her, she'd say he's not impressed with Beth and Noah eye-fucking in the aisle right in front of them. She feels rude because she has no idea what his name is, and she thinks maybe they're both being used, but she doesn't have time to think about it because Beth is dragging him away.

"Are you embarrassed?" Liv asks when they've turned down a different aisle. Noah's arm drops from her waist.

"Ugh," he groans, squeezing his eyes shut.

"Was it worth it?"

"Are you kidding?" Noah asks. "She's so jealous."

"If you like her that much, why do you want her to be jealous?" Olivia asks. She's never quite understood that—the whole "so in love one minute, but the second they break up it's as if they never had feelings for them at all" thing.

If he truly loved Beth, wouldn't he just want her to be happy?

CHAPTER ELEVEN

O livia switches the straightener off. And then she checks they're switched off. And then she tells Steph to make her double-check before she leaves the house that they're switched off.

Steph groans from the other side of the phone. "Ugh, my watering can broke." Olivia can only see the side of her face and a light glow from her Switch, but she knows she's playing Animal Crossing, because it took over their lives during their first summer at college. Olivia's gardening tools only lasted half her vegetable patch thanks to the borderline thief of an Island helper Tom Nook.

"Stephanie."

"You can't just make my name longer when you're annoyed with me," Steph says with a laugh, finally turning to face her. "I made her up myself! There is no Stephanie!"

"Steph-a-roonie."

"You're a child!"

"Steph-a-rono," Olivia says with a smile.

"Yes, I will remind you about the straightener you've turned off seventy times," Steph replies with an eye roll, but she smiles back at her all the same.

Liv doesn't feel bad forcing Steph to be on the phone with her as she takes two hours to get ready, because she helped Steph get through the first few months of her transition wardrobe. Saved her, really, if she had to write a quote about it.

"I feel like wearing a dress to a house party is for if you're under twenty-one," Liv groans, twisting her dress to fit her body. She'll never understand why most of her party dresses require at least another person to get them zipped up. (It usually ends up with someone helping her take it off, but that's neither here nor there.)

"Well, what's the vibe?" Steph asks, half paying attention and half back to building her watering can on her game. It's Liv's fault, really. Liv bought it for Steph's twenty-third birthday—she had to wait in line for the yellow one.

"Er . . ."

"Okay, you didn't ask. So, what are you there for?"

"What do you mean?" Liv asks as she twists in front of her mirror. It's not like she thinks the dress looks bad, and honestly, she would rather be overdressed than underdressed. But there's a time and a place for a strapless leather dress, and it might not be tonight.

"Well, Noah asked you to be his girlfriend for a reason, so who's the girl?"

"*Oh*, Beth. She'll definitely be in a dress, but I'm not about to compare myself to her all evening. I don't know her, and—I'm just going to ask Noah what the vibe is."

Liv takes a quick photo. It's not the best and the lighting is unflattering, but she forgets to care before it's already sent along with the caption "What's the dress code, dicko?"

"Did you tell Noah trying to make someone jealous was going to backfire on him?"

"Mm-hmm," Liv replies, slipping her dress off and putting some blue high-waisted jeans on instead. "But him embarrassing himself is one of my favorite things."

"Uh-huh," Steph says with a tone Liv can't read. She spins to face the phone, pulling her top over her head. She's hoping to see something, because Steph is incapable of keeping her true thoughts off her face, but by the time she's straightened out her top, Steph is still playing Animal Crossing, pulling up carrots. Three at a time. Nice.

Next Door Annoyance: **Well, I'll definitely find an excuse to see you in that dress sometime soon.**

Next Door Annoyance: **But it's more casual than that.**

Next Door Annoyance: **You look great though.**

Her smile pushes at her cheeks without her say-so. She pulls her lip between her teeth, and she doesn't even realize it's happening. She would be happy not knowing she's cheesing over a very vague compliment from Noah for the rest of time she gets ready, but as luck would have it, Steph is done with her game.

"What are *you* smiling at?" she asks with a tone Olivia tries to ignore as she texts Noah back.

Liv: **Mkay. 8 still?**

Next Door Annoyance: **I'll knock on your wall, baby.**

"Ugh," Olivia groans, loud enough for Steph to turn her head again and hopefully loud enough for Noah to hear next door. She didn't even know he was in—he could have been here to help with her clothing dilemma firsthand.

"What?" Steph asks. "Noah too cute and too nice for you?"

"*What?!*"

"I'm just asking a simple question," Steph replies, her full attention on Olivia now. Liv doesn't like it—Steph's narrowed eyes and pouty lips really make it seem like she could just reach through the phone and shake her. Like she knows Olivia had a slip-up earlier, thinking about how it would be to actually be his girlfriend. Like she knows she thought about how the jam would taste on his tongue.

"Will you at least tell me when you fall in love with him?"

"Oh my God," Olivia groans, throwing herself back on her bed. "You're the worst!"

"I know, but you love me," Steph replies. "You know who else you call the worst?"

"Stephanie . . ." Olivia warns.

"I'm joking, I'm joking! Besides, I don't want you to not pick me up tomorrow. What's got you so worked up?" Steph asks, and Olivia usually tells Steph everything—at least, everything she is comfortable thinking about in her own mind—so, she tells her.

"I called him 'baby.'"

"Noooo," Steph replies, cackling as she does. It's too dramatic, but it makes Olivia laugh all the same.

"Shut up!" Liv says as Steph sits up.

"You don't even like pet names! You make everyone call you Olivia!"

"I don't make you call me Olivia," she groans.

"I'd ignore you either way, and besides, I don't count. When did you come up with baby?"

"Listen—" A knocking on her bedroom wall interrupts that thought, and she sighs. "I've been summoned. Tell you about it tomorrow."

She gets up, straightens her jeans out, blows Steph a kiss, and reaches to turn her tablet off. "I'll text you when I'm home."

"Wait, wait, wait!" Steph shouts, and Olivia almost falls over with the urgency of her tone.

"What? Are you alright?!" Liv drops her hand, slapping it against her thigh instead of scooping her phone up as she'd planned. She thinks she looks a little like a forgotten puppet with the way her limbs float around.

Steph smiles at her, a devious little thing.
"Did you turn your straightener off?"

CHAPTER TWELVE

L iv grabs her bag. It's significantly smaller than her summer beach bag, so she can only fit her bank card, ID, phone, keys, and two tubes of lip balm in it, but it's cute and pink, so she doesn't mind.

She checks her hair once more, though there's nothing really to check. Whenever she straightens it, it behaves mainly as she would expect. It's shiny, though, so she flips it over her shoulder as she breathes out to calm herself down.

She's not nervous about going out with Noah. They've been to house parties together before. Well, not *together*. Even if everyone always mentioned that they went together and not with other people, it was never like that. They turned up together because they lived next to each other—it just made sense. Besides, Olivia never wanted to date in high school because high-school boys are a little grim, and no one wanted to date Noah because, well, he's Noah.

But she's always anxious about meeting a large group of people she's never met before. Especially in her hometown, because Liv and her parents were nearly the only Black family in this tiny seaside town for the longest time. She was never acutely aware of being the only black girl in a group—she never noticed at school—but the second she moved to college and saw people that looked like her roaming the hallways and not just online and on TV, she became more aware of how different it is here.

Either way, she tells herself she looks great (true) and that it'll be fun (unsure) and she does a quick tequila shot (possibly regrettable) then pulls her front door closed.

Noah stands in the hallway, leaning against the wall outside her apartment. It's a strange phenomenon—the slight slant of his legs, the way his ankles are crossed, the way only one of his shoulders touches the wall, and the way he's looking straight at her. It takes her breath away a tad. Maybe it's his tanned skin somehow glowing in the harsh fluorescent hallway lights. Maybe it's the way the sleeves of his white top are stretched over his biceps. Maybe it's the way he's looking at her. Maybe it's the single red carnation he holds in his hands.

Maybe it's the tequila shot. She'll blame it on the tequila shot.

"Is that for me?" she asks, finally taking her eyes off his face, forcing them onto the flower in his hand and not letting them trace the cords of his neck.

"Yes," he replies, though his eyes are narrowed. His eyes drop down her body, and she thinks he lingers in places, but she won't call him out on it because she knows he caught her looking at his arms. "Maybe I'll keep it though."

"Ah, the perfect date," she jokes, rolling her eyes as she leans against her closed door. "And why is that?"

"Well, you kept something of mine." He shrugs.

"What?" she asks, her eyes narrowing as he smiles. He loves to say half-thoughts just to wind her up. He mentions something he *knows* she's going to want to know because it's frustrating when she doesn't have all the facts. Half the time when he finally tells her, after hours of her asking, it's a useless statement. He fancies pasta for dinner or something. But sometimes, it's a half-decent bit of information that she's pretty sure he's not actually supposed to have told her. Like in tenth grade when he told her Liam kissed Ashley at a party even though he was dating Emma.

It was always a joke at school—if you told Olivia or Noah something in confidence, it would always be kept that way. Apart from when they told each other.

(Olivia made Noah tell Emma what he saw, but she let him get away with an anonymous note in her locker. Emma broke up with Liam in the middle of the next lunch break, and it's all anyone at school spoke about for the next three days, until someone came to school wearing a bright orange hat.)

But now they've grown up a bit, she's noticing more things about Noah that seem to have changed. Mainly for the better, even if she won't tell him that. So maybe now, he'll just tell her what he's talking about.

"Secrets," he whispers, walking closer. He snaps the flower stem in his fingers, and one—rude. Two—attractive.

(She's regretting the shot a lot right now.)

He places his hand above her head on the doorframe, towering over her. He's always been taller than her, ever since they were kids, but not by this much. She swallows as he pushes her hair over her ear, placing the carnation snuggly behind it. She's not convinced that will stay there all night, and she wants to joke that they're not on a tropical island—they're just strolling down the road to his friend's house—but her joke gets stuck in her throat when he trails his fingers down the side of her throat.

"I *will* be the perfect date."

"Uh-huh," she wheezes. She pushes him away, if only so she can breathe a little easier as she walks in front of him toward the elevator. She'll just have to see it for herself.

Noah barges her out of the way when they get to the entrance of Aaron's house. It's unnecessary because the gates are double their height, and they clearly only open on command, but it's something they've done whenever they walk somewhere together. Olivia just assumed the girlfriend benefits would start soon.

"This is fancy as fuck," Noah states, shoving his hands into his pockets as he leans his head back to see the height of the fences. "Maybe we should have dressed up more."

"Noah." Olivia groans as she looks down at the outfit she decided on. It's just high-waisted blue jeans and a baggy white crop top. The top was actually Noah's, but he doesn't know, and she runs her finger over the flower behind her ear—oh, maybe he does know. Noah is wearing black trousers that she thinks are jeans—but she would need to feel them to check, and she doesn't need to be that close—and a burgundy Nike sweater that he threw on over his white top. (She thinks she should get it—as girlfriend privileges.)

"I'm kidding, baby." He winks as she rolls her eyes at him. The gates creak open, and she pretends she's not intimidated by this house.

"What?" Noah laughs, pulling her closer as they sway down the road. They're not even drunk yet, but Noah is incapable of walking in a straight line, and this time, she's included in his movements because his arm is around her neck.

"What's wrong with baby, baby?"

"Firetruck," she says back, but she laughs as she pushes him away lightly. He lets her go, and that's not what she meant. She just doesn't want to be reminded of her embarrassment at the store all night. But him being half a step away does mean she can walk like she hasn't had eight to twelve drinks.

They walk the long stretch of the driveway in silence bar the occasional sound of a taxi dropping people off behind them. It's comfortable, like it always is. The only thought Olivia has in her mind is that she'll be a bad girlfriend, even if it is fake.

When she broke up with Brendan, he suddenly had a long list of things Olivia did that were wrong, that annoyed him, that he placated because he thought she was pretty. And she hadn't noticed doing any of them.

He didn't like that she commentated films, and he hated that she drew everything in sight, because he thought they should be in the moment—whatever the fuck that means. He was always desperate to meet her parents. She's not sure he liked her at all.

"I don't know how to be a good girlfriend," Olivia mutters, playing with her fingers.

"What?" Noah asks, stopping in his tracks. His brows are high, and she's not sure why. Being a good girlfriend isn't something that would come naturally to her. He would know that, surely. They're so close to the house that she can hear the music being played. The whole scenario reminds her of a typical American house party she sees in movies. She hopes it's not that crowded, but she can deal with drinking from a red cup and half-dancing while leaning against the wall.

"I just—" She moves her hair out of her face for the fif-teen-thousandth time. "What do you want me to be like? What do you want me to do?"

"Just be yourself."

"Noah," Olivia sighs, looking to her side as he steps closer.

He lifts her chin with his hand, his fingertips pushing her hair from her face. His hands are soft against her cheek, and his slow movements are polar opposites to the way her heart suddenly thumps in her chest. She looks up at him, his eyes full of something she can't place. He's closer than he has been since they were paired up in spin the bottle in ninth grade. She feels as lightheaded as she did then, but this time, she doesn't have a chance to move away. She's not sure she wants to.

"All you have to do," he whispers, "is be yourself. Okay?"

"Okay," she replies, trying to make her voice match his, but she hears the breathiness in her tone. He doesn't call her out on it.

"We don't have to go," Noah states, sliding his hand from her face and down her arm. He links his fingers with hers, and she believes him. If she wanted to leave, he'd take her to go and get pizza. But there's a look in his eyes she can't decipher, and she never actually wants to let him down, so as the music switches tracks and the thumping bass rings in her ears, she squeezes his hand.

"Come on," she says. "I'll beat your ass at beer-pong."

The house is even more intimidating on the inside. Olivia grew up with money, she knows that much. They were never going to be homeless, and she had food in the fridge, but it was nothing like this. There's no jealousy, but she does stare wide-eyed as she looks around the grand foyer and through to the room that she thinks is a living room, but she's pretty sure she just saw one on the other side of the house.

She'd feel out of place here, with people she doesn't know and surrounded by decor that's probably more expensive than her entire apartment, but she finds it difficult to feel anything but at home when Noah rubs his thumb over the back of her hand.

He's good at being a fake boyfriend, and they haven't even seen anyone yet.

"You alright?" he asks, pulling them through a crowd of people. It's obnoxiously loud, but she hears him. She squeezes his hand because she doesn't like the sound of her voice when she shouts, and she's not sure he could hear her anyway.

"Hey, man." Noah smiles, his voice loud as Olivia takes her place next to him. He keeps hold of her as he slaps his free hand with Aaron in front of him, doing some handshake Olivia doesn't understand.

"Hey, Noah. How's it going, man? Oh, who's this? *Olivia?*" he asks, a little friendly but also a little predatory. She stands a touch closer to Noah, but he misses her movement, pulling her closer too. She's practically latched to his hip, and her head feels a little dizzy that her hand is splayed across the taut contours of his stomach.

"Aaron, you know Olivia from high school—she's finally home. Oli, you remember Aaron."

"The one you were dreading coming home?" Aaron asks, his brows furrowed.

"Dreading?" Olivia says, turning to look at Noah with a pout. It's mostly playful. She uses the movement to back away a step.

"What can I say?" Noah laughs, pulling her closer again. "Absence makes the heart grow fonder."

"Alright." Aaron shrugs, his attention taken by something behind them. "Not the vase! Sorry, guys. Drinks are on the side."

She watches him leave, her eyes immediately drawn to the colorful array of drinks on the kitchen worktop. She walks toward the drinks, pulling Noah behind her this time.

"You're so full of shit," Liv says with a laugh, pausing at the counter.

"I missed you, Lils." Noah sighs, his head back like a war widow. He keeps her hand in his as he pulls her further into the kitchen with him so he can properly peruse the drinks selection. She doesn't mind because she doesn't know anyone here, and she likes the idea that she won't get left by herself, even if she is stuck with Noah for company. Olivia stands on her tiptoes, placing her chin on Noah's shoulder—she wants to look over, to see what drinks they have, if there's anything bright pink and sugary-looking—but he's somehow grown even more since they were nineteen, so she can't see anything at all.

Noah grabs himself a beer, popping the cap off with a separate bottle of beer. It's unreasonably attractive, and she can't even pinpoint why. He riffles through a selection of other bottles, but her heart is on the bowl of pink punch.

"The pink one," she states, tapping his side with her fingers. She thought he'd know that about her—but maybe she's slipped into the relationship too easily to remember that it's all fake.

"You're so desperate to visit the dentist." He laughs as he pops the lid off a fruit cider. It will do.

"I have great teeth," she replies, smiling brightly at him as he hands her the bottle.

"You do," Noah agrees. He's close. He's always close, but it feels different now. Like the tequila has unlocked the part of her brain that finds him stupidly attractive and she can't think about anything else. He's always been attractive; it's not something that surprises her. But there is an edge to it tonight. There's something somewhere in the back of her mind that wants to think about what him being attractive means.

"Let's find the games," he whispers against her ear. She thinks he lingers, his lips against her ear a beat too long, but she chalks it up to wishful thinking as he pulls her toward the game room.

CHAPTER
THIRTEEN

Noah grabs the beer-pong table just as a game ends. It's one of his specialties, being so tall—he can spot a table emptying from a mile away.

"We can try and find another couple," he suggests, getting new cups from the stack next to the table. "Or we can play each other."

"You're awful." She laughs, but her attention is taken by a loud voice.

"We'll play."

Olivia recognizes that voice, and she's not amused that now she appears to have a spark of jealousy surging through her veins. Liv knew she was Noah's fake girlfriend, and she didn't even want to be that, but she forgot there was an entire reason behind it.

"Sure." Olivia smiles at Beth and her boyfriend. "Sorry, I didn't get your name earlier?"

"Oh, hey, I'm Mark. Nice to meet you."

"Mark, can you get me a drink to play with?" Beth asks, sickly sweet. It reminds Olivia that she wants something sweeter to play with.

"I'm not playing with cider. I'll bloat like a motherfucker," Olivia states, looking back at Noah. He doesn't seem too bothered by the fact Beth wants to play, or that she's even here. She wonders how he's dealing with it much better now, when at the grocery store earlier he looked as though he might pass out.

Maybe he also has liquid courage surging through his body, like she does. Something warm that trickles through her bloodstream and down to her fingertips. Something that makes her want to run her hand down Noah's arm. She doesn't, obviously. But he has pushed the arms of his sweater up to his elbows, so she's struggling to keep her hands to herself.

"You're not having the pink stuff," Noah states as he arranges their cups into a triangle formation.

"I forgot I asked for your permission on what to drink." She scoffs and goes to walk away to grab something from the bar—it might be pink, it might not—but Noah holds on to her wrist. It's gentle, but she knows she wouldn't be able to get out of it unless she asked him.

"Oli," he commands. She turns to face him, his face softer than his tone suggested. To anyone else at the party, they might look like a couple who just needed a moment alone.

J.S. JASPER

Her entire body is touching his, but she feels like a live wire for all the wrong reasons.

"Yes, dicko?"

"You don't know anyone here. You can't trust anyone here. You can't just drink from a communal bowl that anyone could have put anything in."

"Noah," she sighs. "I know you. I trust you."

It's supposed to prove him wrong. It's supposed to show that he's incorrect with his words, and it's supposed to get her the pink drink. But he works with her words better than she can.

"Yeah," he whispers, pulling her closer. She hasn't been able to read him all evening, not really, but right now, it's obvious what he wants. "So let me protect you."

"Noah . . ." She swallows, thick and heavy, and she hopes her body doesn't brush his with the action. She looks up at him, his eyes flicking over her face as she breathes him in. Whatever she was going to say gets lost once again as she sees the determination on his face. He'd never let someone hurt her. Not when they were eight and he was half the height he is now—he'd still put himself between her and the road in case a rogue car going at four miles per hour mounted the curb and flattened her on the spot—and not now.

98

"Please," he whispers, his nose brushing hers. She can smell the beer laced with his words and feel the way his hand rests at the low of her back, and all the fight leaves her.

"Alright. Okay."

"Thank you," he mutters, pressing his lips to her hairline. He lets her go, and she's not sure how she gets to the kitchen still standing. She's not sure how he's allowed to have this effect on her now. She's also not sure how to stop it.

"Yes!" Noah pumps his fist in the air as Olivia sinks another ping-pong ball into Mark's cup. Noah, for his part, has been useless, but she likes how happy he is whenever they don't have to drink either way.

He pulls her to him, wrapping his arm around her shoulders as she laces hers around his waist. They spin together, a silly celebration they've adopted since the second cup vanished on the other side.

It might have something to do with the four they've had to drink as well.

It's Beth's turn. She spins the ball in the glass of water they provided to avoid dipping a muddy ping-pong ball in any of their drinks. It wouldn't matter; Beth and Noah are made for each other in terms of being god-awful at beer-pong.

"I have an idea. Whoever wins," Beth starts, her predatory gaze locked on Noah, "the captain of their team can kiss whoever they want."

Ah, Olivia gets it now. It's all about the chase. She's never been into that—running after someone who either doesn't want to be caught or is so obsessed with the chase that when they finally settle down, they're completely different to who they were before.

But she doesn't blame Noah for liking the challenge. She'll even help him win. Olivia is an ace shot.

Noah pouts. "We don't even have a captain."

"Hey," Liv says with a laugh. Noah looks over at her, laughing with her before she's even said her joke. It's something they've done whenever the word captain comes up. They watched Captain Phillips together years ago. The film was traumatic, and Olivia did not cope well with the idea of pirates stealing a ship, even though that's not going to happen to her because she can't even get on the local ferry. But she couldn't sleep either way, so Noah kept doing phrases from the film in ridiculous voices until she was laughing so hard she couldn't breathe. Now, it's a tradition she hadn't realized she'd missed for the four years she was away.

"Look at me," he whispers, and he points his fingers at his eyes, then to hers and back again. He's moving toward her. "I'm the captain now," he replies, his voice comically low.

She throws her head back in laughter, and she thinks it's not even that funny, but she can't help herself. Noah's arms are around her waist, spinning her slowly as he laughs with her.

"Excuse me," Beth coughs, her arm high with the ping-pong ball still in it.

"Oops. Baby . . ." Noah slurs a little as he turns to look at Liv. "Baby, do you want to be the captain?"

And she thinks yes because then she doesn't have to watch him pick Beth to kiss. Only because then she'd have to pretend to be the jealous girlfriend who is acting like she's not jealous when really she wants to rip Beth's hair out. That's the only reason.

"Not your baby," she whispers, if only to make him roll his eyes and push his tongue between his bottom lip and his teeth. It's a little more difficult to breathe when he does.

She wonders what she'd do if she was captain. She'd have to pick Noah, even if everyone at the table knows he wouldn't pick her back. The thought makes her stand up straight, pushing Noah away slightly.

"You can be captain," she says with a smile. He narrows his eyes at her, but it's playful. She thinks.

Beth misses her throw.

Olivia is ninety-nine percent sure it's on purpose.

Olivia has to down the next drink, and she can smell that it's not the cranberry vodka she picked up earlier, it's tequila. She reaches for Noah's hand, squeezing tightly as she downs it in one. It's not much more than a shot in the cup, but it tastes like college regrets and late nights all the same.

She blinks rapidly when she places the cup in their stack. They only have to sink one more ball and they've won. Beth and Mark have three to go. But as with every game of beer-pong she's ever played, the last ball is the hardest. It's Noah's turn, and by all accounts, he's the weakest link. She's been keeping them afloat from the start—but this all relies on him.

"Focus up, baby," Olivia states, turning to face him.

"Oh, so you can call me baby, but I can't say that to you?" he asks, his hand against her waist.

"Tell me you don't like it," she whispers, lacing her wrists around his neck.

He laughs, a strained sound forcing its way up his throat. For a small, tiny, barely noticeable moment, her eyes fall to his lips, and not for the first time, she wonders what it would be like to kiss him.

She thinks back to the ninth grade when they played spin the bottle and she spent the entire twenty-three seconds it was spinning hoping that it fell on Noah. It's not something she'd allowed herself to think about before, the thoughts only creeping into her mind when she was asleep, or daydreaming, or he was close by.

But then the bottle slowed, and it landed right on him. She doesn't remember the hoots and the hollers as he got up from his space. She doesn't remember the way he looked nervous as he crossed the circle. All she remembers is the terror that if this went badly, she'd lose the only person in the world that cared about her, even if it was laced in petty arguments and hair pulls.

She remembers saying firetruck. She remembers the way she embarrassed him, even though that's never what she wanted.

Olivia is brought back to the present by Noah squeezing her waist.

"You okay?" he asks, his eyes tracking over her face.

"Yeah," she whispers. She's too close, so she smiles and takes a step back, clearing her throat and willing her heart to settle the fuck down.

"It's your shot," she says. "Your kiss depends on this, so don't mess it up."

It happens in slow motion. The way Noah's throat tenses as he swallows. The eagle-eyed focus he has on the cup he wants to reach. The pulse of his fingers as he throws the ball. She's not sure she's ever seen him this determined before. And there it is again, the shallow pit of jealousy that has no right to be taking up space in her stomach. But as she looks at him, at the strain in his arm, the jealousy sets up camp right then and there. It practically brought artwork to hang on the walls.

She watches as it soars through the air, the only time it looks like it might actually be on target. Olivia wonders if she could feign an injury, if she could say her ankle gave out and that's the only reason she nudged the table. But then the play would be taken again, and she'd have to relive this eternity-in-six-seconds all over again.

The ball bounces on the rim of the cup, and Mark lunges for it. The rule is that once it bounces, the other team can swoop in to get it. Olivia recognizes the look on Mark's face—the panic in his eyes as he stretches his arm. As he wishes for something he knows he can't have.

Noah's arms are up in the air, his feet leaving the floor as he cheers. The ball hits the liquid in the cup, and they win. Olivia joins in the celebrations a moment later. She's sure Steph would call her out on it if she were here, but luckily for her, no one here pays that much attention to her.

"I can't believe you claimed the winning shot!" Olivia groans as Noah spins her for the hundredth time. She holds him closer, burying her face into the crook of his neck because she feels nauseous and not because he's comfy.

"It was all you, baby," he replies. And she thinks maybe she should have thrown a few shots, but she'll be over whatever this drunken jealousy is tomorrow anyway.

Her feet hit the floor, and he's the first thing she sees when she opens her eyes. She spins to look at Beth when she clears her throat.

"Alright," Beth drawls. Her body language suggests she's defeated, but her eyes are locked on Noah, keeping him on the hook. Olivia mainly feels bad for Mark. "You won. You can kiss anyone you want."

Olivia slides her arms down his chest, pushing him away with her fingertips.

"Go get her, champ," she says with a smile.

His palms catch her hands before she can fully move away. He pulls her closer, and she can't hear the crowd, the scoffs from the other side of the table. All she can hear is the faint sound of Noah's breathing, barely noticeable over the thumping in her ears. Her eyes flutter closed as his nose touches hers.

"Hey," he whispers, his lips brushing hers. "Can I kiss you?"

She almost jolts at the question, even if everything about him pulling her closer suggests he was going to ask. The only reason she doesn't move is how tight he has her held to his body. She lets the question settle as she comes up with the answer. It shouldn't take her long.

Because no, obviously he can't kiss her. They are frenemies, and they *don't* kiss. He pushed her into a pool in seventh grade, and they don't kiss. He rolls his eyes seventy percent of the time she's in his presence, and they don't kiss. She barely likes him on a day-to-day basis, and they don't kiss.

He's ridiculously pretty, and they don't kiss.

It's decided. She's going to say no, as soon as she forces the word out of her throat . . .

"Yes."

It's slow, the way he somehow moves closer. The way his lips slot softly between hers. The pressure is barely noticeable, apart from the way her knees almost give out. It's not world-shattering; it's not fireworks behind her eyelids. It's comfortable, and it's safe, and it's everything she never realized she was missing.

And then it's over, and she wishes it wasn't.

He pulls back, just slightly. She can feel his heavy breathing more than she can hear it. She knows his actions mimic her own.

"Okay?" he asks.

She keeps her eyes closed, wanting to stay in the moment for as long as possible. His thumb rubs over her jaw, and her eyes finally flutter open.

He looks unsure, and she doesn't like that look on his face. It's the only reason she kisses him again, just a quick peck on the lips. She holds his face in her hands as she feels him smile against her.

"Yeah." She swallows. "That was okay."

CHAPTER FOURTEEN

"I t's er, the nineteenth of August," Aaron says, looking up from his phone. He's been looking for the date of Greg's party for the past three minutes, clearly getting distracted by a stream of texts while he does. Olivia is having a good time tonight, and the thought of doing it again with Noah isn't the worst idea in the world. Especially since his knee keeps knocking against hers whenever he sees someone with a backward cap—a game he decided twenty minutes ago they were going to play. She's losing, but he is a head taller than her, so she's not sure why she agreed to the game anyway.

Besides, she at least knows Greg from high school, so she'd be able to mingle with other people if she wanted, even if deep down she knows she'll be with Noah all evening anyway. (She knows Aaron as well, but he's gotten a little too interested in her for her liking.)

"No can do," Noah states, taking a sip of his beer. "It's Oli's birthday."

And, oh. Yeah, she guesses it is. But she never wants to do anything anyway, even if Noah, Helen, and Joe did make her. It usually coincides with Helen's birthday, which is a few days before hers. She certainly wouldn't want Noah to miss out on her account.

"Ah," Aaron replies. "You'll still be together by August?"

Olivia frowns, wondering if Aaron is even Noah's friend, or if his wanting Beth to be jealous was strong enough for him to be here with people who clearly don't have his best interests at heart. "Because I don't know, man . . ." Aaron laughs, though there's an obvious strain to it, his eyes on her like they have been the entire time. "Liv seems too cool for you."

She's not sure where Aaron is getting that information from because she hasn't said a word to him the entire time, and the only time he's seen her, she's been wrapped around Noah. Maybe he has a humiliation kink. She's not about to shame him, but she's over his obvious lust for her.

"Oh, please," Noah replies, pulling her closer to him with his hand against her hip. She leans her head against his shoulder. "Oli is the amalgamation of every person she's ever thought was cool."

And listen, he's right, but does he have to be so loud about it? It's the first time she's heard anyone talk about her like that, though. As if they understand her on a level she barely understands herself. She's not sure she likes it.

"Oh, shut up," Liv replies, slapping him playfully on the chest. He grabs her hand before she retreats and presses his lips to her knuckles.

"She's the girl next door," Noah continues. She tilts her head to look at him, taken aback by how serious he looks. She guesses he is right—she literally is the girl next door, when she's not away for college—but there's something in his tone that lights a fire in the pit of her stomach. A small fire, but a fire nonetheless.

"She was entirely out of my league, as she is now, and she hated me. So, obviously, I was enamored by her."

"I did not hate you," Olivia groans, feeling the effects of the tequila shots swimming through her system. Or maybe she's still feeling the aftershocks of Noah's kiss—she's trying not to think about it. She's ignoring his words because the thought of Noah as anything other than her annoying neighbor who's around even when she doesn't want him to be is not something her brain can handle right now. Not when he's this close, not when he looks as good as he does, and not when he looks at her like he's looking at her now.

"Tell that to Jason," Noah says, his brows high as she searches her brain for whoever the fuck Jason is.

"Who on earth is Jason?" she asks, and he gasps, his hand on his chest as he does.

"It's a good thing you're pretty, or I'd never forgive you," he whispers, his eyes glistening. From this distance, she can see the green specks in his iris.

"Laying it on a little thick, don't you think?" she asks, leaning away slightly as she sips her drink. It's gotten warm and watery now her ice has melted.

Noah laughs. "I don't care what these guys think. Besides, I didn't lie—there's never going to be a day when you're not out of my league."

"Obviously," she replies, but the lie feels like it's caught in her throat. Liv doesn't care about "leagues" because they make no sense and are based entirely on how someone looks. She mainly cares that someone can make her laugh, and make her feel safe without making her feel like she's weak and needs protection. Being hot is just a bonus.

A bonus Noah has, if she had to think about it.

Noah squints at her, his eyes glassy, and she's nervous she may have said that last part out loud.

"May I help you?" Olivia asks, rubbing her thumb over the dips in her glass. She doesn't want to drink anymore. She's probably drunker than she has been in a while. But she likes how grounded the glass makes her feel, because there's something to do other than loll her head back against the wall and watch the lights dance against Noah's cheekbones.

"Your hair," he mutters, pulling a strand between his fingertips. He pouts.

"You don't like it?"

"It's nice, because you always look nice—"

"Loser."

"Shh," he says with a laugh, leaning his head toward her like he's going to tell her his deepest secret. "Where are the curls?"

"I killed them," she whispers. He gasps, his eyes watery as she laughs. He's adorable when he's tipsy.

"But I like them wild."

"Lucky for me, I don't care what you think," she whispers, tampering down her smile. She doesn't care if he likes her curly hair. Truly.

Maybe a little bit. Like eighty percent does not care, and twenty percent does (but only due to the aforementioned alcohol, naturally).

Noah laughs at her, but it's not unkind. He's never unkind. He's just annoying and always around. Liv finds she doesn't mind that as much tonight.

"Mkay," he replies, placing his empty beer can down so he can play with her fingers.

Okay. So, maybe it's more like fifty-fifty.

CHAPTER FIFTEEN

"Oli, can you calm down, I'm helping," Noah mutters as he stumbles across her bedroom. He drips a little water on the floor, and he tilts his head to look at her, then he looks back at the floor and says "sh."

Liv's just grateful she didn't end up with the water all over her bed.

Honestly, they're lucky they made it home at all with how much they drank at the party.

Olivia giggles. "You're getting my floor wet."

"I'll get you wet if you're not careful," Noah mumbles. His eyes spring open, the flannel dripping onto the floor as she laughs.

"I didn't—not like I *will* get you wet—I mean, I *could*, but that's not—"

"I know." She chuckles, then says, "As if you'd be able to anyway."

It sounds flirtier than she intended. She was supposed to be scathing and mean so he'd roll his eyes at her, because that's their whole thing. But it fell flat, and he's looking at her with a challenge in his eye. His cheeks aren't pink like they are when she's jokingly mean to him. His jaw is set, and she thinks she won't stop him if he wants to prove himself.

But he swallows, sitting on the bed next to her instead.

"Not like this," he whispers, mostly to himself, she thinks, and she lets him keep his words. But the air is charged, and her chest feels like it's ballooning under the weight of it all, and she needs him to look at her like he doesn't even want her here anymore. She needs him to fix something she's pretty sure she started.

"I'm going to have to replace the carpet, you know," she says. It's an olive branch. The best olive branch she has, and thankfully, he takes it.

"Oh, would you calm down." He laughs. "As if you don't sit in this exact position for forty-five minutes after your monthly reset shower. Lay down, please."

"Shut up." She laughs and pushes his leg with her hand. He bats her away, holding her hand down with his as he wipes the flannel over her face.

The flannel is too wet, but it feels nice. She feels the water droplets running over her temple and into her hair. She's not entirely sure she's not being waterboarded, but it's difficult to care when his hands are so soft against her face. His fingertips sweep across her hairline to try and catch the water.

But he's helping, and he's kind and he's soft, and he's *nice*.

"You're going to be a great doctor," she whispers.

"Yeah?"

"Yeah. The children are going to fight over you."

"No one fights over the doctor that has to give them medicine," he says with a laugh. She's not sure if he's dropped the flannel on the floor, but it's no longer dripping onto her face, and she finds she doesn't mind all that much.

"Who cares about the medicine? They're all going to be arguing over who gets the cute doctor."

"You think I'm cute?" he asks, but before she can answer, his eyes widen, and he throws himself forward. For a moment, she thinks he might accidentally headbutt her, so she screws her eyes closed, waiting for the impact that never comes.

"Jason?!"

Olivia tries to spin to see what he's talking about, but he sits back down, his free hand still on hers and his other with a fistful of teddy bear. Her bear, whose name is Vincent—not Jason.

"You kidnapped him." Noah pouts. She has little to no idea what he's talking about because he gave her the bear for her birthday years ago. "I tried to find him when you went to college, but I thought you'd thrown him out."

"I took Vincent with me," she replies. "Is this the Jason you were talking about at the party?"

"Vincent?!" he asks, ignoring her entirely. "When did you change his name?"

"Noah," she says with a laugh. "You gave him to me for my birthday. He came with no birth certificate that said his name was Jason."

"I did?" he asks, his brows furrowed. "I knew I wanted to give it to you for Valentine's Day when we were like, twelve, but I chickened out. I just—I don't remember your birthday that year."

"Well . . ." She swallows, ignoring the fact he wanted to give her a Valentine's gift because she can't handle that thought right now. "Your mom gave it to me, but it was labeled from you."

"Oh, that little wannabe matchmaker." He laughs. "I guess you never hated me after all."

"I never could," she replies, the truth hanging too heavy in her dark room, so she throws a smile on her face. "Even if you're the worst person I know."

"Ha. But, the question remains, Oli . . ." He slurs a little as he tucks her bear under the covers with her. "Do you think I'm cute?"

"I said the children will think you're cute," she clarifies with a smile.

"Ah, of course," he says, nodding his head rapidly. His hand is still on hers, not so much holding her in place anymore, but it's there. She moves her fingers slightly to rest them between his, but the movement seems to spook him.

"I better . . ." He gestures with his thumb toward the window. "You know Mom can't sleep until I'm back home."

"Please don't go out the window."

"Lil," he moans, leaning forward until his head rests on her chest.

"You tripped on my floor and it's flat."

"But—"

"Nope," she replies with a pop of her lips. "Firetruck."

"You're so—" He laughs, running his hand through his hair. "Fine, you menace, I'll trek home."

"Dramatic, and for what, baby?" she asks, and he squints his eyes at her. He runs his thumb along her hairline once more, then sighs and gets off the bed. She wants to tell him he can stay, but she's not sure she's going to be able to sleep anyway. Not with the thoughts floating through her head.

"Sleep well," he says with a smile, bringing her hand up from the bed to press his lips to the back. She's not a princess in the eighteen hundreds flirting with the farm boy that she's not even allowed to look at, but it sure feels like it.

He pulls the flower from behind her ear, and she's surprised it stayed there all night. She's surprised it didn't get waterlogged with the attempted drowning Noah just did to her. He places it in the glass of water he got her to drink. She doesn't mind.

117

She watches him walk away, flicking her desk lamp off on the way out. When he reaches her bedroom door, she thinks he's far enough away that she can say something to him that won't end in her moving over and telling him to slip in.

"Noah," she says, and he turns to face her, leaning against the doorway. "I do think you're cute."

He smiles at her—a small thing she'll forget about by tomorrow morning, if she can help it.

"I knew it."

CHAPTER SIXTEEN

O livia is not hungover.

But she does sit under the stream of hot water in the shower for far longer than she should anyway. It's not like her to wash her hair twice in one week if she can help it, but when she woke up this morning, her hair was curly in a halo around her face, and the rest was straight, and she simply could not be bothered to straighten it again.

So, she sat in the shower instead. She half crawled out the bathtub to reply to Steph's message about the train being on time without getting her phone drenched, and she refused to eat breakfast.

She might be a little hungover.

She lets her thoughts linger on how her head feels like it might explode and the way she needs to squint even when she's in the house (Does everything need to be so bright?) and the way she regrets drinking so much last night while she gets dressed for the day, instead of letting herself think about Noah.

Because if she thinks abut Noah, she has to remember how they kissed, how he asked to kiss her and she said yes quicker than she's agreed to anything in her life. She'll have to think about how his hand felt in hers, and how she misses it now he's not here and she's not even drunk. She'll have to think about what any of her thoughts mean. Does she like him? No. Does she want to date him? No. Is she sure she's telling the truth anymore? No.

So, she forces herself to think about her headache, even as she feels that fade away as she walks toward the train station because she's going to pick Steph up for lunch. This is the longest they've been apart in almost four years, and that includes the summers when Steph was supposed to stay at home but barely lasted longer than three days.

There's a feeling of dread in her stomach that it might be awkward. Maybe they've been apart too long and Steph has found a new best friend and it might not feel as comfortable as it always has. Maybe she's made it all up in her head and Steph thinks it's weird that she's even coming down for the day.

She tries to shake the thoughts from her head, but if she does, the only other thing she lands on is the way Noah looked under the flashing lights last night.

That's great. Fantastic.

She leans against the wall in the train station because all the benches are taken by people with more luggage than she thinks is reasonable. She likes the train station—she likes to imagine everyone getting on the train is going on an adventure. Maybe they're leaving home for the first time and they're full of nervous excitement. Maybe they're going to their job, and they'll be waiting for five o'clock when they'll see this view again because it means they're coming home.

Maybe it will be like that for Steph. Maybe she's sitting on her chair playing Animal Crossing and she's excited to see Olivia again. Maybe she's regretting the journey because it takes two hours and seven minutes and the last ten of those are a painfully slow stroll into this harbor station.

The worries disappear when she spots Steph through the window of the train. She's standing near the door, her back-pack on, and she looks more like Steph than she has in any of the video calls she's been on in the past few weeks.

Olivia waves at her. Steph flips her off as she walks off the train. And all is right with the world.

Steph throws her arms around her when she steps off the train, even though Olivia isn't a hugger. Steph never cared, not really.

"Hey, baby."

"Noooo." Liv cringes as Steph cackles at her. She's truly the worst best friend anyone has ever had.

"Lets go, you can tell me all the juicy gossip over lunch."

The juicy gossip stays locked in her chest in a place she doesn't want to look. She's not sure what any of it means. Sure, a kiss—a drunk kiss, at that—means very little. It should mean very little. She doesn't even like Noah. But every time she looks into the place in her heart where she keeps her hidden thoughts, it feels like there are snakes in her chest, and she locks them away so fast she feels breathless.

So, she avoids the question about last night Steph asks her once their lunch arrives.

"I got the job," Olivia says casually. She opened the email a few minutes ago when Steph left to go to the toilet.

"You what?!" Steph all but screams. "The one that's actually graphic design?!"

"Mm-hmm," Liv replies.

Steph laughs. "A little more excitement wouldn't be a bad thing, Liv. I know you've still got to decide between the two, but you're acting like someone died."

"I am not," she says with a laugh. It's not like someone has died, of course. But the thought of having to make life-changing choices by herself just seems too hard.

"Are you happy?"

"It's my dream job," Liv replies instead of answering the question. She tears a bit of bread between her fingers.

"Avoidance, but okay. What's the issue?" Steph asks, always so direct with her questions. She's very much of the belief that if there's something Olivia wants, she should figure out a way to get it. It makes sense, in theory, but she's not so sure it does in practice.

"I don't—I can't afford a place here. Not for a good couple of years, anyway," she says. She looked on her housing app the other day (one of her favorite things to do is browse houses she could never afford and judge the owner's decorating skill. An eight-bed house with nine bathrooms, a cinema room, and a massive garden, but the interior is all wallpapered? Not a chance.) and there was nothing even close to her current apartment for less than her monthly paycheck.

"The commute would be hell on earth."

"Liv."

"Mm?" she asks, dipping her bread into the pasta sauce.

"You already live here."

"Yeah, but like—that's my parents' place. I don't want to have to rely on them."

Olivia has told Steph that her parents aren't around much, but not the details. She feels guilty talking about how much she despises them and the neglect when Steph is stuck with a family that won't let her live the way she wants. The way she needs to. The way she was born to live.

"Well, yeah, I get that," Steph agrees. She takes a sip of her water. "But if it helps you out now, why not?"

She thinks about what it would be like to stay there. Would she decorate and make it feel more like home, or is that a feeling she'll simply never associate with that apartment? She figures she could paint it green. Noah would probably help her.

Noah would be there. Well, he'd be around. Probably. Until he moved out of his parents' place. If he gets into the residency program, he'd have to live close by, right? She's not sure what junior doctors make, so she's not sure if he'd have to commute or if he could live near the hospital without going into a deep depression with thirty pounds left to spare after rent.

She could suggest they lived together. Not together, together. Well, *technically*, they'd be living under the same roof. Oh my God, they'd be roommates.

"I could just move closer to you," Liv states quickly, avoiding thinking about Noah being around her more than he already is. She tries to remember that he annoys her if he's around too long. She tries to shove the thoughts of kissing him to the back of her mind. She lets the pasta sauce sit on her tongue for a few seconds before she swallows. Anything to distract herself.

"I still have the other offer. They sent a chasing email."

"Oh, we could live together!" Steph exclaims.

"I kissed Noah," Olivia blurts out. The distraction was as useless as she expected.

"You did *what*?" Steph asks, her eyebrows high as she pauses sipping on her water. It's dramatic in the way everything about Steph is.

"Listen . . ." Olivia laughs, running her fingertips against her napkin. She likes to talk with her hands, and she's not about to be pecked by a seagull just because Steph said they should appreciate the weather and sit outside. (The sun is warm but not too hot, there's the slightest breeze, and they've only had to scare off one seagull thus far, so Liv has to agree that Steph was right.)

"We won a game of beer-pong," she whispers, pulling her lip between her teeth as Steph stares at her. The excuse feels feeble out in the open.

"Why did you even say you'd be his girlfriend?" Steph asks, a look in her eye Olivia does not appreciate. She clearly thinks Liv has been waiting for a chance to be Noah's girlfriend. Rude and untrue.

"I felt bad!"

"You're going to end up pregnant if you do things for Noah just because you feel bad."

"You're so—"

"So, what now?" Steph asks, all but throwing her cutlery onto her plate and pushing it to the side. They only have time for lunch today, and a stroll back to the train station (though Liv will take her through the park first).

"Er—well, we haven't spoken about it."

"Are you embarrassed?" Steph asks. She's always *so* eager to point out how well she knows Liv, even if it makes her blush. "Oh my God, you're not! That's the issue."

"Oh shush." Liv laughs, then pouts at her food. She moves some spaghetti around her plate with her fork. It's a little cold now, and she was full a solid eight bites ago, but she's not ready for the meal to be over.

"I can't believe my train is in an hour and you spent the first half of lunch not talking to me about this," Steph gripes, pulling her phone out.

"I mean, I did tell you about my parents being useless and the whole job scenario."

"Your parents have always been useless, honey—tell me something I don't know. Or at least let me egg them. And you know how I feel about the job—"

"What's the point in getting a job if it's not near you?" Liv defeatedly places her knife and fork together on the plate.

"Exactly! But kissing your childhood nemesis who doesn't sound at all like he actually is your nemesis, now that's the-second-I-get-off-the-train goss!"

"Oh my God." Liv groans, looking anywhere but at Steph. "You're just—oh, come *on*."

Of course Noah is walking past on the other side of the street as she's just finished thinking about all the ways his lips felt against hers.

Steph looks excited, like she can hear Olivia's heart thumping from the opposite side of the table. Like she's just desperate to spin around and scream Noah's name.

"Don't," Olivia warns.

Steph spins her head around so fast Olivia worries she might have snapped a vertebrae. Steph calls him over, and Liv kicks her shin under the table, but it's too late. His head pops up from where he was looking at his phone, and his brows furrow as he looks for who called out to him. It doesn't take him long to see Steph's waving hand. He skips through the slow-moving cars and past the hoards of tourists with a smile on his face.

"Ladies that lunch?" he asks, coming to a pause just next to their table. He doesn't look hungover at all. Prick. He's in the way of people walking past, so he slips slightly behind Olivia's chair.

"Hey, I'm Noah." He waves at Steph.

"Steph," she replies, with a smile and a look. Liv widens her eyes at her to get her to stop, but she just smiles against her straw.

"Ah, bestie Steph," Noah says. Olivia doesn't remember telling him anything about Steph, but he is a stalker, so he might have seen her on her Instagram. "I assume Oli has only ever said nice things about me." Liv laughs. Presumptuous of him to think she talks about him to anyone apart from her therapist.

"I don't lie to Steph, so don't hold your breath," Olivia whispers, looking for something to play with, but she can't find anything, so she picks at her thumb instead.

"So you do talk about me?" Noah asks excitedly, resting his hand on her shoulder.

"All the time," Steph exaggerates. Liar. Fibber. Worst friend ever.

"Yeah?" Noah asks. Liv tries to hit his hand with hers, but he catches it instead.

"Shh, I do not!"

"Like last night, and how you two—"

"Steph!" Liv groans. She needs to think of another version of firetruck, apparently.

Noah laughs. "Last night was fun. So fun, in fact, that we're going on a date tomorrow," he says with a smile. He lets her hand go but he leaves his thumb rubbing against her shoulder.

"We are?" Liv asks, tilting her head to look up at him. He moves her hair from her face, then rests his hand lightly on the back of her neck. She moves her face back when she's blinded by the sun. It's possible she was too drunk last night and has agreed to go on an actual date with him, which would be the worst because he's the worst, but then she remembers how his lips felt, and, well . . .

"You agreed to go to Ryan's party," he replies, his thumb moving closer to the hollow of her neck. It's distracting, and she tilts her head to look up at him again. He moves forward slightly, shielding her from the sun. He's pretty upside down as well.

"Oh." She groans when he smiles that annoying smile at her—the one that he knows winds her up because it means she's wrong and he's right. She moves her neck so she can pout at Steph instead. It's a mistake, because Steph looks like she's figured something out, even though there wasn't anything to work out in the first place.

"Yep. Drunk you is much friendlier than sober you."

"That's true!" Steph says, raising her glass.

"Oh, shut up," Liv replies, reaching to slap Noah's free hand, but he catches her hand before she touches him at all. He twists his fingers with hers and rests it against her other shoulder.

The hand that was resting against her neck tightens slightly, his thumb under her jaw so he can tilt her face back to his.

"Wear something pretty," he whispers, laughing as she rolls her eyes at him.

"I'm wearing a bin bag," she replies, smiling as the waiter places their bill on the table. She reaches for it before Steph can, but Noah beats them both.

"I've got it," he says. He bends down to press hips lips against the top of her head, her curls brushing the sides of her face with the movement.

"You go and be ladies that stroll."

"You don't have to," Olivia starts, but she knows better than to try to get Noah to drop something once he's started.

"Baby," he whispers, just for her, but Steph splutters on her drink enough to know she heard it as well. "I've got it."

"Thank you," she mutters. She grabs her bag from the seat. Noah pulls her hair out from underneath the strap for her.

"Oh, and you'd look great in a bin bag."

CHAPTER SEVENTEEN

"**W**hy don't you two just fuck?"

"You're the most dramatic person I've ever met," Olivia replies, pulling Steph out of the way of a group of tourists with their linked arms.

She groans, throwing her head back. "You're perfect for each other."

Olivia leads her across the road. She wants to show her the promenade before they go back to the train. They haven't got long, though, so she won't be able to linger. They spent too long looking at the flower stall, and they didn't even buy anything. They didn't have any peonies, and they're Steph's favorites. The red carnations were pretty, though, but she still has the one Noah gave her in her bedroom. The ones at the stall didn't seem as special..

"You heard us speak to each other for about three seconds," Liv says with a laugh. The sea is shining under the bright summer sky, and Olivia feels herself settle at the sight.

"Yes," Steph replies, "but I watched you look at each other, and honestly, that's enough to figure it out."

"Uh-huh." Steph is wrong. Noah has always looked at her like that. Nothing seems to have changed for him at all, so she's not sure why she's getting so hung up on one drunken evening. He's completely normal—and she can be completely normal too.

"Why is this so pretty?" Steph asks, dropping Liv's arm to lean her palms on the seawall. She raises her face to the sky.

"I know, right?" Liv replies. "Maybe you should be moving here instead."

"Mm-hmm. If you stay, I'll move so fast," Steph hums. "Even the ferryboats are cute. Do you go on them every day?"

"I've actually never gone on one."

"What?" Steph asks, looking over at her, and then she turns her face back to the sky and closes her eyes. "But they look so fun, even with my eyes closed."

Liv laughs. "Yeah. It's a parental trauma thing."

"Ah, say no more. Maybe you should ask Noah if he wants to go on it. You could get married on one or something."

"Oh my God." Olivia groans. She watches a young family playing catch under the tree. "You're not allowed back here."

"Noah would let me come back," she grumbles.

And he would. He would invite Steph back so fast if she even hinted to him that she wanted to be here. He'd invite her to stay at his place, and then they'd all end up at Liv's anyway. But she doesn't want to ask Noah to go on the ferryboats with her. Partly because he asked her numerous times when they were teenagers, and she always had an excuse as to why she couldn't go. But mainly it's because she thinks it's something she should do by herself. She doesn't want to pick another man just because her dad let her down. She's not someone that needs a guy to do things with her.

"You don't have to need a guy," Steph replies, and Liv wishes she knew what she thought in her head and what she said out loud. She's comfortable telling Steph anything, really, but she'd love to be a little more aware of it.

"I know," Liv replies, feeling embarrassed. She knows that. Somewhere, very deep down, she knows that.

"But you can *want* a guy. That's the difference. You can ask him because you want to, not because you need to."

"Why are you so wise?" Liv asks with a sigh. She pulls Steph from the seawall so they can walk to her train.

"Something about my type-three personality," Steph says with a laugh. "So, you should listen to me about Noah."

"Steph," Liv warns.

It's something she's barely allowed herself to think about. Whether his comments are flirty because that's how he is. Whether or not he's thinking about her as much as she's thinking about him. Whether he's terrified of what it all might mean. Whether he thinks getting involved with her is a good idea—or if it all goes wrong, will he lose the most important person to him too?

"Okay, okay," Steph replies. "I'll let it go. Just think about it! And try to have fun at the party tomorrow. And text me when you get home."

CHAPTER EIGHTEEN

L iv likes to people-watch. She makes sure she's always sitting facing the world when sharing a table with people, and she likes to lean against the wall at parties so she can see what's going on. She's not nosey because she doesn't really care what anyone is up to, and she's not about to eavesdrop when someone looks angry. She just likes to see what's going on around her.

Right now, though, she's a little bored.

The party isn't bad, per se. There are just no activities that include everyone, so if you only know one person at the party, as she does—a person that barely likes her at the best of times and is a menace to society—then leaning against the wall is the only thing to do, even if it's not enjoyable.

It's a little better than worse when Noah is next to her, but she doesn't understand why, and she's not thinking about it right now.

The music is great, though—a subtle nod to the early noughties, with songs she hasn't heard in years. It's cringe in a way all the best things are. She hears the beginning of her teenage soundtrack start with "How You Remind Me."

And *fuck* does she love this song.

"Dance with me," Noah says, moving from his position of leaning against the wall. He spins on the spot when he's barely four steps from her, holding his hand out.

"There's not a dance floor," she states, rolling her eyes as she takes another sip of lukewarm cider.

"Dance with me anyway."

"This isn't even a dancing song." She groans, but he steps closer anyway, then takes her drink from her. Rude.

"Dance with me anyway," he whispers, his nose brushing hers as he places his hands around her waist. He's the most annoying person she knows, but she's never been able to deny him anything, not really.

They're barely moving, his hands lightly against her waist as she tries to ignore the people staring at them. There's hardly any space, maybe a meter or two between them and the couch, but Noah doesn't seem to care. Everything blurs when they dance together. The lights dim, and her entire focus is on Noah's face. If he's enjoying himself, if he's having fun with the slow turns they take. If he's comfortable with the way her arms are laced around his neck. If his face shows any change from before. If there's anything in his smile that suggests it feels a little bit different for him right now.

She doesn't figure anything out, and then it's too late. It's slow until it's not, and their heads are banging along with the tune and that's not the only reason everything in the background disappears and all she can see is Noah.

His hands are everywhere, somehow holding her close so their bodies touch every time they move, they're on her arms and in her hair and everything about how she's feeling right now is centered around Noah.

She wants to know if she can get closer to him if she moves one way, or if she can link her arms around his neck again when the song reaches the bridge. More than anything, she wants to know if he wants that too.

Before she knows it, he's figured it out for her, his arms pulling her close to him as he smiles. She smiles back.

He's not singing anymore, but he asks the question as the song does.

And she thinks yeah, she's having fun. She's always having fun with him.

There's a squeal and a "Watch out!" and she barely has time to turn her head to see what's going on before she realizes something is about to hit her. This is why she likes to watch from the outside, because the chances of getting an entire cup of lukewarm beer thrown all over her by a slippery-footed drunk guy she doesn't know are significantly lower. They're never zero, but she prefers the odds.

She's in the air before anything touches her though. She's hoisted to Noah's hips as he spins her out of the way and back to their corner. There's no one here, which she's thankful for because nothing even happened, but her heart races all the same, and she doesn't want anyone to ask her any questions.

"You okay?" he asks, placing her gently on the windowsill. When she finally opens her eyes, he's standing between her legs. She's not scared, obviously—that would be ridiculous—but she feels a tiny bit sick because of the fast movement and the amount she's drunk. Noah helps, though. He's always got her back, even if she can't see at all.

"I'm good," she says, taking a deep, leveling breath.

He tilts her head up, his fingers light under her chin as he does. His eyes track her face, but he nods his head and starts to move away.

"Stay here," she whispers. It's supposed to be demanding, but it comes out as more of a question than she would like. It doesn't matter, though—he moves back, hooking his chin over her shoulder as she wraps her arms around him.

She buries her face in the crook of his neck and sighs. She's tired, and she feels a little too grouchy over the whole drink situation. Nothing even got on her. All that happened was Noah spun her out of the way, and now she gets to spend some time with just him. So, she's not sure why the rage is hanging out in the back of her mind, desperate to come out. She ignores it as best she can. It's easier when Noah runs his fingers over her spine. Occasionally, he twists her curls in his palm, and she thinks she could fall asleep with how safe she feels here.

But then Beyoncé comes on the speaker and she wants to dance—*needs* to dance—but as she goes to shuffle off the windowsill, she feels an ache in her lower back. She wasn't even sitting particularly weird. Bodies are entirely too rude.

"We can dance here," Noah says, pushing her back onto the windowsill with his hands heavy on her hips.

"We can't," she grumps.

"Oh, yeah?" Before she knows it, he's shuffling in front of her, his shoulders taking it in turns to be comically close to his ears as he moves side to side. He looks ridiculous, and she thinks he might be her favorite person in the world.

Noah has a confidence she'd never have that makes him able to do whatever he wants, wherever he wants. Everyone is just lucky he's the nicest person, so he only ever does things that make people laugh because he wants them to be happy. He'd never embarrass anyone but himself. He doesn't seem to care that people are staring at him with their brows furrowed, whispering to their friends that he's spinning on the spot.

Olivia laughs slightly, hiding her face in her hands as he clicks obnoxiously along with the beat of the song.

He grabs her hands with his, pulling them away from her face as she continues to sway in place.

"You're ridiculous!"

"Doesn't matter," he replies, moving closer as he links her arms around his neck. He settles slightly, his body still moving slowly to the music, but it's not as obvious. He rests his hands against her waist.

"Made you smile."

CHAPTER NINETEEN

I t's dark when they walk home. The party is almost definitely still in full flow, but Olivia was tired, and Noah had
suggested they go home.

"I'm sorry if you wanted to stay later," she says, crossing her arms over her chest. She forgets that nighttime in
summer is still cold. She's used to going home around ten
because she likes to watch the sunset, but she also likes to
be in bed by the time the temperature changes.

"Nah," he replies, his hands deep in his pockets. "Walking
you home is my favorite part of the night anyway."

"Shut up." She laughs and knocks into his arm with hers.
He turns to look at her, his head surrounded by the glow of
the streetlamp. He looks pretty. He always looks pretty—it's
the main thought rattling around her brain at all times. But in
the dark, with the moonlight above them, he looks romantic,
and maybe that's why she drops her gaze to his lips.

She chickens out, of course, but she does take two to three
deep breaths while thinking about holding his hand.

"Let's go, loser," she says, stepping up her pace when the cold air hits her. She moves her hand around, looking for his, but she doesn't find it. Well, that's alright—she takes the hint. But a few steps later, she realizes he isn't with her at all. Instead, she sees him lifting his sweater. She watches as his abs flex when he accidentally pulls his T-shirt with it. She swallows, her throat feeling all too thick.

"It's okay," she says, biting back a shiver as he pulls the jumper off his shoulders. Her eyes are definitely still on his stomach. "I'm not that cold."

He rolls his eyes at her as if there would ever be a way he'd let her get away with not taking it.

"Noah, I don't want it," she says with a laugh, backing away from him, his eyes dark as he follows her.

"I'll catch you," he whispers, and his words turn her on more than is reasonable. She wants to blame it on the alcohol. But she'd always let him catch her anyway, so she doesn't complain when he's in front of her, her back against a tree trunk, and she's glad no one else is out here.

"You'll get cold," she replies, her fingers against his chest, and she feels warm as his eyes roam over her body.

"Oli," he says, his eyes lingering on hers. "I'd willingly die for you. I can be a little cold."

"You're the most dramatic person I've ever met," she whispers, but she lifts her arms when he motions for her to.

"I'm your favorite person in the world," he replies. His fingers are cold against her neck as he pulls her hair from the collar of his sweater.

She finds she doesn't want to lie to him. Not today. So, she doesn't tell him that's not true.

"You're not getting this back," she says, pulling the cuffs of his burgundy sweater over her hands, letting the tips of her fingers lace with his.

"Mm. Looks better on you anyway."

"Does that mean I get free rein?" she asks. "Because I've been eyeing up that cute navy blue tee for weeks."

"You're a menace! You chop them all up anyway."

"I do not," she replies, then . . . "Well, the ones I sleep in are still full-sized."

He lets out a moan she feels deep in her chest. "How are you allowed to sleep in my clothes but I've never even seen it?"

Olivia barks out a laugh as she walks toward their apartment. "I'll send you a photo."

"No takebacks!" he shouts, jogging to catch up with her.

"I can't believe you didn't bash me out the way," Liv says as he walks into the apartment elevator behind her.

"I'm a very polite boyfriend," he replies, leaning against the back wall. She's standing slightly away from the wall, so now she's not sure what she wants to do. Should she slowly edge back until they're standing next to each other? Should she stand her ground and if he didn't want to stand next to her that's fine? Should she even be overthinking something like this? Her mind has been all over the place today, and she can't figure it out.

So, she does the only thing she knows how to do with Noah. She's snarky.

"*Fake* boyfriend."

"Fake boyfriend," he repeats. She can hear the smile in his voice, even though she's refused to turn around. She misses him, even though he's right here and it's ridiculous. She's letting herself be ridiculous in her mind—no one can judge her there. Well, apart from herself, but she's not sure she likes herself right now anyway.

She shuffles on her feet. She's not wearing heels, so it makes no sense for her entire body to be achy simply because she's been standing still for two minutes. She should have leaned against the wall as Noah did. Fool.

Besides, she thinks her comment has left a sour taste on the evening, and she's not sure how to fix it. Before she winds herself up by the fact that she's suddenly uncomfortable both physically and with Noah, something she doesn't like to be, his hands are around her waist, and he pulls her back to him. It's only a few steps—three, max—and she thinks she should have just done it herself, but she's thankful for him anyway.

She leans her back against his chest and she doesn't try and hide the way her breath is choppy when he presses his lips to her shoulder.

"I can carry you," he mutters when the elevator finally comes to a stop. Olivia isn't sure if she fell asleep in the few moments between the first floor and the fourth, but she feels comfortable enough in Noah's arms that it's entirely possible.

"I want to say yes so badly, but imagine if Mr. Davids comes out of his apartment and catches us?" she jokes. Mr. Davids is a prude. A rude prude who often leaves his apartment just to chastise people in the hallway. Whenever her parents were actually around, they'd say it was just because he was old and from a different time. Liv thinks he's just a prick.

"You're so right." He laughs, pushing her out the elevator doors. His thumbs feel nice at the base of her back, so she lets him maneuver her until they're outside her apartment.

She fishes her keys from her purse and spins to look at him. It's different now that he's dropping her off. It feels more real than it has before, and she has to remind herself she only ever agreed to be his fake girlfriend. He only ever asked her to be his fake girlfriend.

But as he drops her home, she feels something settle into her chest. The certainty that it's not fake for her. She's not sure it ever has been.

She can't tell him that. Not right now, maybe not ever. Because if he doesn't feel the same way, she loses everything about him. He'd be kind, of course. He wouldn't tell her to stay away. He wouldn't tell her she'd done anything wrong. But it would be different. The familiarity wouldn't be there anymore. He wouldn't share things with her, and she wouldn't be able to share things with him because all her thoughts surround him.

Instead, she simply says, "I had a nice night."

Noah smiles at her, a soft smile that he only lets out when they're alone.

"I had a nice night too."

"Good."

"Good."

"Cool."

"Cool." Noah laughs.

"Uhm . . . So . . ."

Her keys almost slip through her fingers.

He leans forward, his hand on the door frame above her head, and she tries to stop herself from moaning. She's only semi-successful, but he doesn't call her out on it.

"Do you wanna come to a mixer with me tomorrow?" he asks, his voice low. There's no reason for him to be this close just to ask her to go out with him tomorrow, but she's not about to ask him to move.

"Do you ever stay at home?" she replies, her voice breathy, as she tries not to let her gaze fall on his lips. Going out three times in one week? What is she, twenty-two?

"Ha," he whispers, his nose brushing hers. "It's for the residency program."

"Yeah?" she asks, leaning on her tiptoes just slightly. She's not sure where her bravery has come from, but her lips barely touch his as her eyes flutter closed. She feels his smile against her lips and moves her hands to rest against his chest. The jingle of her keys does nothing to lessen the thump of her pulse in her ears.

"Mm-hmm," he hums, as he slots his lips between hers. His hand slides up her arm and over her shoulder, finding a home at the back of her neck. It makes her break out in goosebumps, and she clings to his top. He tugs at her hair while his other hand lingers by her chin, his thumb pulling her bottom lip down ever so slightly.

"Oli," he whispers, his words vibrating down her throat, finding a home in her chest. She traces his lip with her tongue, but just as she's about to ask him to come inside, a door clicks open, and Olivia knows her night is about to get cold water poured all over it.

"Young people never know how to behave," Mr. Davids croaks from behind his door. He's loud enough they can hear, but it's probably not enough that the neighbors will come out and look at what he's complaining about this time. (If they left their couches every time he raised his voice, they may as well live in the hall.)

Noah clears his throat, pulling away from her a touch, and she lets him.

"Good evening, Mr. Davids."

He grumbles, shuffling in his darkened doorway. Olivia wonders if he stands on a stool to stare out of the pigeon-hole in his door, desperately waiting for someone to dare hold hands with someone they haven't been married to for forty-five years.

"I'm just dropping my girlfriend home, and I'd appreciate a little privacy," Noah states. He's still close, his hand resting at the nape of her neck, though he's dropped the other from her lip.

"Noah," Liv whispers. "It's alright." She's never been one for confrontation, even if it comes in the form of a five-foot-two, pushing-eighty-year-old man who looks like he might fall over in a soft breeze.

Noah looks at her, his eyes dark as she rubs her lips together. She won't fight him on it if he chooses this moment to stand his ground—if this is the time he wants to call Mr. Davids out on his annoying self-appointed role as the nuisance neighbor. But she's tired, and her back hurts for no reason at all, and she wants to sit in her room and sort out the thoughts in her head. The ones that are telling her to tear Noah's top off in the middle of the hallway, and the ones that want to sketch every iteration of his face. The ones that are telling her to ask him to stay for the rest of time, and the ones that want him to kiss her again. And the ones that are trying to remind her that this was all supposed to be fake.

But of course, he doesn't fight her on it. He gives her what she wants, as she thinks he always will. He kisses her once on the forehead, his hand tight at the back of her head to hold her close.

"Sleep well, Lil."

Olivia pulls her—or Noah's, she guesses—T-shirt on as her pajama top. It's soft, and it's her favorite one. It's baggier than all the others because she got it from him when he just got out of his over-the-top-big T-shirt phase, so it hangs off her shoulder. She thinks back to when he was walking her home, and she wonders if sending him a photo is ridiculous. If her saying that was clearly a joke and he won't think anything else about it.

She's already taken her makeup off, but she hasn't put her hair up yet, so she pulls her camera out to take a test shot, just to see if she actually looks like a ghoul or if the fact she feels swollen everywhere means her face will look flushed.

When the phone screen lights up, she sees Jason out of the corner of her eye, so she grabs him and positions the bear so it's covering half of her face. It's nothing scandalous, not really, but it's nothing she'd post on Instagram.

The photo ends up being eighty percent hair, a bit of her smiling face, Jason, her bare shoulder, and Noah's T-shirt. She ruminates over sending it for a few minutes but then hears him shuffling in his bedroom and she wonders what he looks like. So, she thinks "fuck it," writes a quick message, and presses send.

Her heart beats rapidly, and she wonders if it was all a mistake. But then she hears him fall on his bed with a groan, and suddenly, she's smiling at no one, and she doesn't mind at all.

Her phone lights up moments later with a text from him.

Next Door Annoyance: **I miss you both too.**

She thinks she might change his contact name.

CHAPTER TWENTY

Olivia wakes up feeling like she's eaten an entire whale. Well, actually, she *looks* like she's eaten an entire whale—she's actively starving to death. It's barely nine a.m., but she fancies a burger, or maybe a salad because she did want to get back into healthy eating, but she also deserves to eat what she likes because it's her life so maybe she should have a burger for breakfast.

She barely opens her eyes before the bright sunlight from outside her bedroom makes her want to throw herself down a set of stairs, or maybe she wants to go for a walk along the entire coast of her town. She's only ever done it once with the Grants, years ago, but maybe she should put her playlist on and just do it.

She sits up, the pain in her lower back spreading into her bum, through her legs, and into her stomach. Excellent. She's dying. But then she stands up and she feels it, the trickle between her legs that turns into a gushing stronger than the high tide on the promenade, and she knows she has about three seconds to run to the toilet before she ruins another set of underwear.

Her period is here. Right on time, as it is every twenty-eight days, and just like last month, she forgot all about it.

It makes sense now—how tired she was last night, how grumpy she was over an almost spilled drink. How she may as well have shoved her tongue down Noah's throat in front of Mr. Davids. She'll probably get a notice from the landlord about public indecency. She wonders if anyone's ever used having their period as a defense in court.

Liv wakes up from her second nap of the day wrapped in a blanket that makes her feel too sweaty and with the wires of her electric heat pad twisted through her legs. It's a stark contrast to the dream she was having that may or not have involved Noah, and now she can't let him into her mind lest she burst into flames.

So, she shakes her head, throwing him out of her thoughts and moving on to the rest of the day. Ugh. She's going to need to have another shower before she gets ready to go out tonight. She thinks about what she could possibly wear that won't make her look seven months pregnant. (She's sure if her mom had been around for any time at all, she should have told her that being bloated on her period is more in her head than it is in her body. Or she'd tell her that bloating isn't the worst thing in the world, because her mom was—well, is—never around, but she sure was wise whenever she was.)

Still, she gets out of bed and wraps her hair up into a tight bun because she's not dealing with washing her hair on top of everything else today. Putting her playlist on loud, she texts Steph while the water in the shower heats up.

Olivia: **Got a fancy (I think, idk) event tonight and pbomb decided it would be a time to turn up. Outfit suggestions please (prayer hands)**

The hot water feels heavenly against her shoulder blades, and she almost throws her head back but stops when she thinks about having to get the diffuser out. Anyone would think she had run a marathon and wasn't just dealing with cramps and too much sleep.

She squirts an unreasonable amount of body wash on as she tries to take her mind off the racoon in her ovaries and onto the fact that tonight will be fun. Maybe. Probably not. But it is important for Noah, so she'll suck it up.

Oh, no, now she's let Noah back into her mind. She tries to stop it, but it's no use. All the thoughts are flying around her head, and she can't make any of them sound friendly. Steph says she could just ask Noah if anything has changed for him since they started fake dating (not even fake dating full time, he might be real-life dating someone else and she'd have no idea). She could ask him if he was dating anyone, fake or not, or if things with Beth are progressing as he wished—or if maybe he thinks about her as much as she thinks about him. But what if he didn't? She'd be so embarrassed that she'd have to cut him off permanently, and she likes him a little too much to chance that.

She's like forty percent sure he likes her in the way she likes him. Sometimes she looks at him and he's already looking at her, and it makes her feel like she's stood up too fast, but anytime she gathers up the courage to tell him about it as they sit at the park, all the insecurities from high school come roaring back.

How she was the weird one with no friends who didn't get asked to prom. (She went with Noah in the end, but he never wanted to ask her, not really.) Or the way she was the only person whose parents didn't show up to the parent-teacher conference. The only guy that's ever been there for her through everything is Noah, and she's had twenty-three years (maybe eighteen, if she lets her five-year-old self off the hook) and she hasn't done anything about it.

There's also the possibility that if she tries to tell him one thing, she'll start with the little things—like how she wants to wake up with him, or how she likes it when his hair is curly because he clearly didn't have time to flatten it that morning. But then it will snowball because she has no filter around him, and she won't be able to stop so she'll tell him how she thinks about him all the time and how she wants him to stay for the rest of his life and how she's thinks she's falling in love with him.

And they're thoughts she doesn't even let herself have in the dark in her bedroom, because they're terrifying.

So, she shuts the water off, banishes all thoughts of Noah from her mind, grabs her phone, and goes to start getting ready. She likes getting dressed up, and she likes doing her makeup—it's therapeutic.

"Oh, for fuck—" She throws her eyeliner onto her desk.

Steph laughs from the other side of the phone. "I told you." She did in fact tell her not to try eyeliner when she was "in this mood." Unfortunately for Olivia, her "this mood" swings from *she can do whatever she puts her mind to* to almost crying within about three seconds. She called Steph the second she got out of the shower because her suggestions for what to wear were unhelpful, to say the least. She's sure Steph only suggested lingerie and nothing else because she's bored at home, and not because she thinks that's something Liv would like to show Noah.

"Ugh." She sighs, wiping the corner of her eye again with a makeup wipe. She'll be lucky if it doesn't start bleeding. The rest of her makeup is fine. Just fine. Her bronzer won't blend out properly, even though she used it yesterday and it was entirely fine. Her eyebrows are barely cousins, let alone twins. But she doesn't have time to redo it all, so she's hoping a bit more blush and some setting spray is going to fix it.

She swallows and takes a deep breath. It's just makeup.

"Just tell Noah you can't go," Steph says, her voice kind. She's always said she's so glad she's a girl without periods because they sound life-ruining, and she's not wrong. Sure, on day three, Liv could go to a fancy function and be fine. Day one might kill her off.

Liv laughs, though it's strained. "It'll only be a few hours and then I'll be back with my heated blanket."

"Mm-hmm. When you finally tell him—wait," Steph says, sitting up in her bed. She places her hand over the speaker on her phone, muffling the voice from whoever just strolled into her room. Liv can barely hear her mutter something to someone, and her heart sinks—she wishes she could get her out of there.

"I've gotta go. Show me your outfit and text me when you get home."

"Okay, are you alright?" Liv asks, though she knows she'll say yes either way.

"Yeah," Steph replies, though her smile doesn't reach her eyes. "Love you."

"Love you."

The phone clicks off, and Olivia sighs. She's been complaining all day because she's tired and her body aches just a bit, and Steph has been having the worst time and she—she feels guilty. Steph would tell her to shut up, that just because someone else is struggling doesn't mean she can't be having a bad time as well. But still, it sits heavy in her chest.

She stands up and fluffs her hair. She could look *worse*. Olivia decided on a burnt-orange satin dress because it's her color in summer and it hangs in a flattering way (it's a halter neck with a low cut back that pools just below her waist. It's her favorite). Noah knocks on her wall as she shuffles it down her body. There's a tussle to get her pajama shirt off through the straps of the dress, but she wins. Only just. She can't get the button at the back of her neck done up because *of course* she can't.

Noah climbs through the window as the struggle between Olivia and the dress continues. He walks over, his fingers taking over for her. She feels as though she can't quite catch a breath all of a sudden. As if he might be able to feel how hard it is for her to exhale while he does her up.

"There you go," he says, his voice low. He pulls her curls from under the straps, letting her hair hang behind her back.

"Thanks," she whispers. She swallows, spinning around, and—*holy shit*. She's seen Noah in a suit before, at a family wedding and at prom, but that was different. Sure, her throat still ran dry when she saw him, but now there's feelings she can't attribute to anything other than the way he looks at her and the way he's unreasonably kind and the way she wants to hold his hand.

"Holy fuck, Oli," Noah exclaims. "You look amazing."

"Shh." She groans, pushing him away, but he doesn't let her. She's never been particularly good at accepting compliments, and it's worse now she wants it to mean something. It's worse now she wants him to want her the way she wants him.

"Never," he whispers, twisting a curl around his finger. "You're so beautiful."

"Thank you," she manages to get out, shuffling on her feet. She needs to grab her heels. "You look great too."

"Thanks," he replies with a smile, his eyes still floating over her. It makes her feel as hot as she did in her dream.

"Mm-hmm."

There's a period of silence, and suddenly, she doesn't know how to fill it. She used to wish he'd be quiet for just a moment, and now he's giving her the time she so desperately wanted and all it makes her think is that he can hear the fireworks in her chest when he looks at her.

"What time is it?" she asks, spinning to gather her things from her desk. Olivia shoves a couple of tampons into her bag and some painkillers. She takes some deep breaths as a particularly painful cramp starts somewhere deep in her bum.

"Er," he starts, pulling his phone from his pocket. She watches the screen light up, and it takes her breath away when she sees his background is her. Thankfully not the photo from last night, but another photo he must have taken when they went to the park last week. She looks from the phone up to Noah, but he's preoccupied with sliding his phone back into his pocket, so she's not sure he sees her.

"What?"

He squints at her. "I said it's six twenty-four."

"Oh, okay, we should go then."

"Are you alright?" he asks, holding on to her wrist. His fingers are chilly against her skin, and it feels phenomenal. She wants to ask him to rest his palms against her back, but she's not sure she'd be able to deal with him physically touching her right now.

"Yeah." She smiles. Yes, it feels like there is a racoon in her ovaries, and yes, she thinks her uterus might fall out of her vagina at any moment, but she's good.

"Fibber."

"Excuse me?"

"When you lie, your left eyebrow goes up."

Olivia sighs. "You could get arrested for those stalking skills." She's not a fan of people knowing more about her than she knows about herself, but she figures Noah has earned it.

"Lil, what's wrong?"

"I just have my period, no big deal." She shrugs. It's not like she's nervous about telling him because it's a taboo subject—she's not thirteen, and neither is he. She just doesn't want to spend twenty minutes convincing him she's fine to go tonight when she doesn't really want to leave the house and she hates to lie to him.

He sits down, pulling her with him, but she manages to remain standing. If she sits down with him right now, there's no way she's getting back up again.

"Why didn't you say?" he asks, his brows furrowed. "We don't have to go."

"It's not a big deal." She shrugs. "Besides, you look so good in this. I shouldn't be the only one who gets to see it."

She runs her finger along the collar of his suit, watching his jaw clench from the corner of her eye.

He chuckles, his hands loosely against her hips. "I fear I should be the only one to see you in this." It's a streak of possessiveness she's never really heard from him before. It makes sense that she hasn't, because she's not actually his.

160

Even if they did date, she'd never *be* his because she's a whole person who doesn't belong to anyone.

It doesn't stop the swooping feeling in her stomach though.

"That's a shame." She laughs, letting her fingers linger near his throat as he looks up at her. "I've already shown Steph."

Noah laughs, throwing his head back as he widens his legs. He pulls her closer, her knees touching the edge of her bed.

"Tell me something," he says, and she barely clamps her teeth closed in time to stop from replying "Anything."

"Would you ask me to go if I was in pain?"

"Noah," she sighs. "That's different. It doesn't hurt anyway, and it happens a lot—I can deal with it."

"I had a headache for like three weeks in high school and you refused to let me go to school *and* did all my homework so I didn't have to open my eyes."

"So?" She laughs. She goes to walk away with the intention of dragging him out of the house, if only to see him in his suit under as many different lights as possible. She reaches for his hands, and he gives them to her but doesn't budge.

"So we don't ask each other to do things when we're hurt. Promise me you're not hurting, and I'll get up."

"Noah," she replies, rolling her eyes. She can't lie to him—because apparently he has her face mapped out—but she knows this is a big deal for him, and she can take some more painkillers in like two hours.

But it's too late; he's taking his suit jacket off.

"We can just go for a little bit!" Liv states, trying to pull his jacket back over his shoulders.

He stands up, letting it fall to the floor, and holds onto her hands.

"Change into sweats. I'm ordering pizza."

"Bossy." She steps closer, though it's not necessary—she may as well be standing on his toes.

"This is important for you," she mutters. "I can go, or I don't mind if you want to go without me. I'll get pizza for when you get back."

He scoffs. "You're crazy if you think anything is more important to me than you." He presses his lips to her nose like he's telling her the menu for a casual dinner and not words that make her feel as though she's walking a tightrope. "Crazy, crazy girl. Now change, please. We're staying in."

CHAPTER TWENTY-ONE

O livia spends far too long thinking about what to change into. Noah went to the shop to grab some snacks to go with the pizza he's picking up on his way back, and she's spent the entire time trying to decide if she should put pajamas on or if she should wear something nicer. She's not sure what would constitute nicer and still look casual enough to be lounging around her house.

She texts Steph to tell her she's not going out but they are staying in, so if she wants to call, Liv's available. Steph told her to finally put the lingerie on. Liv ignores her, mainly. She does put some cute comfy underwear on though. It's just black, obviously, but it flatters her. It's not like she's planning on sharing this information with Noah, but she doesn't feel bad about her decision. (She also decides on her comfy shorts and a long-sleeved black top.)

Olivia tidies up her bedroom, putting her makeup away and making sure her bed is made. She potters around the living room, fluffing up pillows and refolding blankets. She manages to dust the television and unload the dishwasher before she realizes she misses him. It's barely been twenty minutes and she misses him.

He's funny and unfairly kind; she's not sure how he missed any of it before. Well, she didn't. She always knew he was nice, and she always laughed at his jokes, it was just over-shadowed by everything else. Her insecurities and his pity and personality. It's easier to focus on how much she might hate him to avoid focusing on how much she might not.

Also, he holds her hand, and it's a simple touch, but it makes her feel all the better. So she lets herself miss him. She sits on the bar stool, leaning her elbows on the kitchen counter, and she sighs like her husband has gone to war and she doesn't know if he'll return.

Noah's back moments later, and she feels a little pathetic but she lets herself off.

"I got chocolate and cornflakes," he shouts as he kicks the door closed. He's looking through his bags (her bag—he stole her tote, but she'll let him get away with it) and when he looks up, he smiles as he sees her sitting there.

"Hi."

"Hi," she replies, trying to ignore the butterflies in her stomach and the thoughts in her head that surround him always coming home to her. The thoughts that they could be a real-life couple, that they'd go to the grocery store together and they'd fold laundry together on the couch instead of doing it in the laundry room.

"I got cornflakes and chocolate," he repeats, at a lower volume this time. He places the pizza on the side and pulls the food from the bags. "I thought we could make cakes."

"Yeah?" she asks, walking around the counter because he's too far away.

"Mm-hmm. You like baking when you're down, but I can't bake to save my life, and I didn't wanna give you something else to think about—so how hard can cornflake cakes be?"

"So easy," she says with a laugh. She goes to pull the juice from the bag, but he bats her hands away. She watches him pull a plastic mixing bowl from the cupboard and leans forward to press her lips to the skin of his neck, feeling giddy when he immediately spins to face her. His lips are slightly parted and his eyes are bright, though he doesn't say anything. So she bites his shoulder too.

She goes to move back to her safe place, the place where she only thinks about climbing him like a tree but probably won't try and fuck him in the middle of her kitchen, but he's quicker than her, and he pulls her back to him with his hand on the back of her neck.

"Hi," he says.

"Hi."

"You missed me," he whispers, his lips dangerously close to hers.

165

"Yeah," she replies, swallowing as his thumb rubs over her cheek. "Is that okay?"

"It's the best fucking thing, Oli."

He lightly presses his mouth to hers, chuckling when she chases his lips as he moves back. She hears the bowl drop lightly to the side as he pulls her face between his hands.

"I missed you too."

"Well, obviously." She laughs as he takes a step away.

They grab the mixing bowl and the wooden spoon, and Olivia watches the tendons in Noah's arms as he snaps the chocolate into pieces. They opt to melt it in the microwave because boiling water sounds too much like actual cooking right now.

He fills her bowl with milk chocolate and adds white chocolate to his bowl, then they add a borderline-obnoxious amount of cornflakes to each. It's alright if they don't eat them all. Grams's party is tomorrow; they can always take some spare.

"Oli?" Noah asks after a period of silence, though his shoulder touched hers every now and then.

"Mm," she replies, stirring the cornflakes into the melted chocolate.

"Where are your parents?" he asks. Rude. She thinks a trigger warning before family questions should be added to their relationship rules, but she lets it slide because she loves him or whatever.

"I think my mom is in the country." She frowns. She should know that.

"Yeah," he replies, "but when does she get back?"

"Erm, well, she usually turns up for your Grams's party, so, tomorrow?" she says.

"I know they're not around all that much." He laughs, but it's strained. "But you don't even know where they are?"

"I haven't seen them since before college."

Noah spins to face her with so much force she holds onto her plastic mixing bowl like her life depends on it.

"Wait, *what*?"

"You can't be shocked, Noah." She laughs, though she's embarrassed at his questions. Usually, she'd tell him to fuck off and stop being so nosey, but now she's letting him in and she's not sure she likes it. "I never saw them when I lived here."

She watches it all play out on his face. The way she was always over. The way she'd cry on the phone and he'd hear it through their shared bedroom wall. She'd tell him it was a sad movie and to mind his own business. He never did, and she hated him for that, but she can't find it in herself to hate him now.

"That's why you spent the holidays with us?" he asks, his voice cracking, and she wants to roll her eyes because he's overdramatic, but the look on his face stops her.

"Mom became head of her department years ago. She was never able to stop working, and I can't ask her to just because I was alone—"

"Yes, yes you can."

"Noah," Liv starts, placing the bowl down so she can rub her thumb and forefinger against the bridge of her nose. "She's the first Black woman to be head of her department. Ever. Besides, I liked spending time with Helen and Joe."

"And me?" he asks, like he's not truly sure of her answer. As if he's not the only one she ever wants to annoy her.

"Barely." She smiles.

"But it got better, right?" he asks, borderline begging, and she knows it's because there was a summer in ninth grade when she stopped going to their house. After all, she overheard Noah complaining on his headset with his friends that "she was so annoying and unlovable." She still went over for Sunday dinner because saying no to Helen was too hard, but she dropped out from holiday events early and went to their spot alone.

"What?" she asks, flustered by his string of questions.

"You stopped coming over for a bit when we were teenagers, and if you stopped because your mom and dad were here, that's great, that—" He swallows. "But if you stopped for me."

"Noah." She sighs, then says, "We were children. It's fine."

THE LAST GOOD THING

She never wanted him to feel guilty, even though it's clear he does. She never wanted him to treat her any differently than he would if he thought she had two parents who wanted to give her the world. And he knew they weren't around—he must have known that. She never wanted him to feel bad about something he couldn't control.

He wound her up and then gave her some of his fries, and he called her out when she needed it, and he was the only person she knew that was always there, no matter what.

"Oli."

"It's all I've ever known. I'm happy. My mom is useless, my dad is useless, but that's just how it is."

"Liv," he whispers. She hates the guilt in his tone. She doesn't like pity.

"Don't be weird about it," she mutters. "Please."

"I've never been weird a day in my life," he replies, but his voice is off. She won't look at him, though—not right now.

It doesn't matter. Noah is there anyway. His arms surround her before she can push him away. His chest is against her back, his lips by her neck. It's the most loved she's ever felt in this house.

It always is when he's here.

"You wish," she replies, linking their fingers together.

"Success," he whispers, and she wonders why, but it's too late. He's spun her away from the countertop. He keeps spinning as she yelps, and before she knows it, all thoughts of her parents are gone, and she's over his shoulder as he dances them around the living room.

She's trying not to fall in love with him. Really, she is. But she's not sure she ever had a choice.

Olivia remembers putting a movie on. She vividly remembers pushing Noah's thigh with her foot when he suggested watching *Die Hard* for the eight-thousandth time. She almost let him get away with it, too, because she seems to be in the mood to say yes to whatever he wants. But she stops herself when she sees *Notting Hill*. Noah pretends he doesn't like it, but she catches him tearing up when Max makes everyone get out of the car for his wife, because *of course* he's not leaving Bella behind.

She remembers Noah making salty popcorn and her throwing it into his open mouth pretty successfully. (They're definitely going to need to Hoover in the morning.) She remembers Noah passing her the red sour gummy worms because they're her favorites. She also remembers pulling the blanket from the basket she placed next to the sofa, so maybe that's the reason she finds herself in this position now.

The sound of rain tapping at her living room window is what wakes Olivia up. She's confused like she always is when she has a nap she hadn't planned. It's dark in the living room, the lampshade casting creepy shadows onto the walls from the streetlights outside. She tries to stretch out her legs but it's unsuccessful, and she wonders if she's fused in place because she's actually slept thirty-six hours and missed the entirety of the next day. She can't figure it out because she's still so sleepy, the deep ache behind her eyes refusing to disappear even after she scrunches them for the fourth time.

"Wha—" Noah mutters, and her eyes flick open. Noah is lying on top of her, his head against her chest with his feet hanging over the arm of the sofa. She wants to run her fingers through his hair and to know what he sounds like when he's just woken up and to know what he's dreaming about, but he's heavy, and he's practically pinning her to the couch.

Liv tries to sit up slightly. She can barely sleep on a different pillow than normal without waking up in the morning with a broken back. The movement does nothing to make her feel more awake, and Noah doesn't appear to have gotten the message. He wraps his arms further around her waist, pulling himself closer to her. So, she lies back down, her eyes closing again without her say-so. He's comfy.

"Let's move," he says, his voice raspy as he peels himself off her, and she wants to pull him back, to tell him to stay.

171

That it can barely be two a.m. and she doesn't want to spend the rest of the night without him, not now she knows what it feels like to sleep with him. But even in her somewhat sleep-deprived state, she can't ask that of him.

She does grunt when he moves, though, because she'd rather just stay on the couch—she's too tired to move.

"Not happening, baby," he murmurs. He picks her up with ease, one arm under her knees and one under her arms.

"But I'm so comfy," she groans, leaning her head against his chest.

"Mm-hmm, but you can't abandon me for the party setup tomorrow when you can't walk because you spent the night on the sofa."

"Stop knowing so much about me," she grumbles.

"Never," he whispers, dropping her lightly on her bed. "You're my favorite thing to learn about."

She'll dissect that tomorrow, when she has more than one brain cell functioning.

He pulls her socks off, which is rude because she loves to sleep in socks, and he tucks her into bed. If she were more awake, she'd pout at him because she's been in this outfit all evening and she doesn't like to get into bed in the same clothes she's been wearing. But she didn't leave the house, so she thinks she'll let him get away with it.

"Stop pouting at me." He laughs, pushing her lips back with his fingers.

She finally opens her eyes as she laughs with him. Her room is shrouded in darkness, but she'd find him anywhere. He's sitting on the edge of her bed, looking entirely too handsome. If she'd met him in college, she would have hung on his every word. She kinda wants to kiss him for real, but she's been asleep anywhere between three seconds and seven hours, so she doesn't, even if now she feels the most awake she ever has in her life. She's not sure she's even going to be able to sleep again.

"I can't believe I missed the end of the movie," Olivia says with a yawn.

"Baby, you were out before they even kissed."

"I was?" She groans. What a waste.

"Mm-hmm. I didn't last much longer. I missed your commentary."

"Shut up." She giggles and throws her hands over her face.

"Never," Noah replies, his voice low as he moves a piece of hair from her eyes, and she's clueless as to how she's supposed to function when she knows what he sounds like when he's sleepy. How his eyes take a beat longer to open.

"Noah."

"Mm?" he asks.

"I'm sorry about tonight," she whispers, looking up at him. It's not dark in her room, but she'll think about the way his curls hold the little light there is as she falls asleep.

"There's nothing to be sorry for." He shrugs. It looks like he wants to say something else, but he doesn't, and she's not brave enough to press him on it.

"What time tomorrow?"

"I . . ." Her breath sounds choppier than she would like, and she thinks she can see her duvet move with the rapid beating of her heart. Noah can definitely see it, but he doesn't call her out on it. His hand has found a home at the base of her neck, his fingers twisting her curls, almost enough to tickle her. It makes her feel like a live wire. "I guess, like nine?"

"Okay," he replies. He drops his lips to her forehead, his hand spreading against the pillow she's lying on. His thumb rubs against the pulse point on her neck, and she tries her best to level her breathing. "Nine it is."

He can stay if he wants, she thinks. But ultimately, she watches as he closes her bedroom door.

CHAPTER
TWENTY-TWO

T he sky is bright when Olivia wakes up. It's earlier than she expects, because Murpheisn't having his mid-morning sleep on her fire escape yet.

She blinks the sleep from her eyes, knowing that going back to bed is a waste of time. She slips out of bed, feeling gross for falling asleep in a long-sleeved top. Olivia walks to the bathroom to brush her teeth and wash her face. She feels better today. Her period is barely a thought beyond tampons, and she feels like she can think coherently again. She contemplates taking a shower, but the grumble of her stomach takes her back to her room.

She kind of wants to get pastries and tea and sit by the promenade. She kind of wants to go with Noah. But as she looks at her phone, she realizes it's already ten a.m., which means she's missed Murph's snooze and all the breakfast pastries will be gone already, and she was supposed to meet Noah an hour ago.

She sits on her bed as she scrolls through her messages. Three from Steph saying how she doesn't think she needs a job, actually, someone should pay her just to live. (True.) And one from Noah. She can't help the smile that blooms on her face when she sees his name.

NDA (heart emoji): **Sleeping Beauty, text me when you're up x**

She knocks on his wall instead and hears him shuffling around his room a few seconds later. His window goes up, and she's grateful for his vague disrespect for deathly fire escapes because it means she doesn't need to wait for him to walk the forty-seven steps from his bedroom to her apartment door. Olivia pulls her window open, the warm air hitting her face.

"Morning," she says with a yawn when she hears him climbing through his window. She can't see him yet, but she pushes up on her tiptoes so she can see him faster.

"Sleepy girl," he says, sounding much more awake than her.

"Mm. I missed the opportunity for breakfast. Beware."

"Oh, no!" He laughs, pulling himself to the corner of the fire escape, and sits down cross-legged like he has no fear the structure could fall to the ground at any given time. He's so far away. "I'm not dealing with a hangry you."

He pulls a paper bag from his bedroom, and even from her room, she can immediately smell the pastries.

THE LAST GOOD THING

"Oh my God, did you go to Josie's?"

"Mm-hmm. I thought you'd be tired," he replies. He opens the bag fully, holding the paper open with two takeaway cups in his hands.

"Tea?" she asks.

He smiles. "Of course."

She crawls out of her window, feeling more nervous with every slight movement she makes onto the fire escape.

"Um, I changed my mind," she says nervously, but she can't figure out how to turn around and return to her room.

"Here," he replies. He moves with ease, leaning against the fire escape closest to her room. He lifts her by her waist and drops her in his lap. She spins slightly, hanging her legs over his thigh, her feet practically in her bedroom.

"Is that alright?" he asks, bending forward to pull their food closer.

"Yeah," she whispers. "It's great."

She settles against his chest, taking the tea from his hand.

"Grams asked if we could get there around three to help decorate, but the party doesn't start until seven, so we could get ready first, go and decorate, and then stay there instead of coming back in between. What do you think?"

"Works for me," she replies, taking a bite of croissant. She wants to work up the courage to ask Noah if he wants to spend the morning with her. They used to spend days together without talking, and it was fine. She used to wake up during summer and Noah would already be in the living room, and it was just how it worked.

But no. Now she knows she might, slightly, be falling in love with him. Now it's awkward to ask him if he wants to hang out. Figures.

Still, she swallows the last of her croissant and rubs her fingers together over the edge of the fire escape so the creatures and the birds can have a tasty treat. She's going to ask him if he wants to go on a walk to nowhere, or maybe she could say she needs to do laundry and maybe he has some he needs to do as well.

"Wanna go to the park?" Noah asks. He's always been the braver of the two of them, or maybe her answer just isn't as important to him as his would be to her.

Oh well. The result is the same anyway.

She smiles. "Yes."

"Oh, for fuck—" Her hairband flies out of her hand and skitters across the floor. The pressure of holding her curls in place as they desperately try to break free was just too much to take. Liv dives into her bag, annoyed that she brought the beach bag for a trip to the park, because she knows she only needs one single hairband, and she has everything in here from tampons to plasters to a charger for her Switch that she left at home and her lip balms, of course, but there definitely won't be a single hairband.

"Here," Noah says, pulling a hairband from his wrist. His hair isn't long enough to tie up. (Liv knows that because there was a period of time when she was sixteen when she was obsessed with long hair and thought Noah had the bone structure to pull it off, but she never told him that.)

"Oh, thanks," she replies, testing the strength of the hairband before she attempts to put her hair in a bun. Sturdy, but not that wide, so she settles on putting half of her hair into a bun and letting the other half hang down her back.

"I love your hair like that," Noah states, his eyes trained on his book. She's not sure he's even reading—his page hasn't been flipped in minutes—but he looks nice and she wants to draw him anyway, so she doesn't call him out on it.

"Is that why you have a hairband with you?" she asks, ignoring the way his words settle into the folds of her heart.

"I've had a hairband on my wrist since the seventh grade," he says, looking over the top of his book at her. "I can't believe you never notice anything about me."

"Don't be so dramatic." Liv laughs, poking him in the side. She catches him smiling out of the corner of her eye.

She won't tell him she noticed how his eyes change color in the sun, from dark brown to hazel. She won't tell him how she missed his nerdy pun T-shirt era when he decided he was too cool for that in the ninth grade. She won't tell him how she watched him take extra Spanish lessons throughout high school because he wanted to be able to talk to Izack, the foreign exchange student who was only in school for a two-week program.

"I'm nothing if not dramatic, Oli." He sighs, his head tilting until he rests on her shoulder.

"Why are you wearing a hairband?" she asks, maneuvering so she can sit against the tree in comfort, her folded-up jumper taking the brunt of the bark for her. She pats her shoulder once she's comfy, but Noah is already moving. She doesn't like it—she wants him to lean on her, but she doesn't know how to ask for it beyond the small hand movements he might not have seen.

It doesn't matter, though, because he drops his head into her lap, the back of his neck hanging over her thigh. She decides this is better.

"Yours snapped during gym class and you were so sad, Lils." He pouts up at her. "So sad because you didn't like your curls back then, and I don't like it when you're sad, so I wore one in case it snapped again, and I don't know, it's kinda just routine now."

She thinks maybe fireworks are going off in the distance, or perhaps there really is a mariachi band strolling through her chest. She can feel her cheeks heating. Noah always pretends he can see it, even with her dark skin, but she thinks he's just winding her up.

She deals with it the best way she knows how.

"Why are you so obsessed with me?"

He laughs, throwing his head back against her thigh as he smiles at the sky. He looks up at her, a look in his eye she still can't place, but she wants to give him the world if only to make him happy.

"It's hard not to be."

CHAPTER
TWENTY-THREE

"I missed you, you know," Noah says, folding his sweater neatly so he can use it as a pillow. Noah always lies on the grass when they go to the park. Liv used to be so jealous when they were younger because he would be fast asleep within minutes, but she can't lay on the grass because it makes her itchy. It did always give her some uninterrupted time to draw, though, and his hair was usually fluffy from the sea air, so she didn't mind all that much.

"When?" she asks, pulling her pen out of her bag. She riffles through it, but she can't find her sketchbook, which is unreasonable because she never leaves the house without her sketchbook.

"When you went to college."

"You did not." She laughs, her head deep in her bag. Fuck, it's not here. But the flowers surrounding the tree opposite are so pretty, the purple upside-down petals of bluebells and the pinks of the tulips that are somehow still standing even though people like to pluck them and now she's in her tortured artist era.

"I did so," he replies, flipping onto his side. His forehead rests against her hip, his body curving around her crossed legs. She shivers, and it's nothing to do with the twenty-eight-degree heat and she prays he doesn't call her out on it. She barely let herself think about actually liking him (if she lies to herself, which she does, and please don't judge her) and if he asks her why she's suddenly nervous around him, she'll probably burst into flames.

He'll laugh at her because this whole thing is fake anyway. It's make-believe, and she's fallen for it hook, line, and sinker. So, instead of indulging him with his comments about missing her when he probably had a party the day she left for college, she calls him out on it.

"You hated me being around. Why would you miss me when I was gone?" It's meant to be light and jokey, because she's pretty sure he never hated her outright, but he did hate having her around. It hurts to ask, though, and she's using all her effort to not think about why that is.

"I did not hate you being around. You're so dramatic," he says, his voice heavy with all the signs of a sleepy Noah, and he's only been lying down for approximately seven seconds.

"You didn't like it," she whispers, twisting the pen in her fingers to stop from doing something stupid like running them through his hair.

"Here," he says, draping his arm over her lap. "You can draw the flowers on me."

"Have you not heard of the dangers of ink poisoning?" she drawls, though she repositions his arm all the same.

"It's a risk I'll take for you, baby," he replies, then says, "I always wanted you around. Why did you think I invited you to things?"

"Helen invited me. Don't think you get the credit for that," she mutters as she sketches out the part of his arm she wants to draw on. It's probably going to go onto the back of his hand, because she'd have an excuse to hold his hand and she thinks about that an embarrassing amount.

"She asked you because I asked her to," he replies. "I never wanted to ask you to your face because you never wanted to hang out with me."

"What?" she asks. "If I never wanted to hang out with you, then why was I always there, huh?"

"Because my mom asked," he says with a laugh.

"Yes, I would indeed throw you under the bus for Helen, but I liked spending time with you."

"You're so rude all the time," he replies, his fingers smoothing over the skin on her thigh. It makes her break out in goosebumps, and she swallows around her sigh.

"You know," she starts, nervous at the words she's about to say. If she thought about it too long, she probably would keep it to herself, but she's already speaking. "Even if we were fighting, you were the only person I cared about enough to fight with."

"Yeah?" he asks, and she just knows he's looking up at her with a dopey look on his face, so she focuses on finishing the sketch on his arm.

"Shh."

"Sign it, please," Noah says, holding his arm out to her again as he takes photos. It's pretty. He's always pretty, but the vines and the flowers wrapped around his wrist and onto his forearm are pretty too.

"Loser." She laughs, but she does so anyway. "It would look nicer in watercolors, but I left mine at college."

"It's flawless. I don't know what you mean," he says, pulling his phone out of his pocket and typing something on it. Maybe Grams wants them there a little earlier. Maybe Beth is talking to him. She decides to not ask.

"Let's go get ice cream before the party," Noah says, standing up and stretching his arms. She doesn't mind the view. He dips back down, looking at her as he riffles through his backpack, then he pulls out her sketchbook and hands it to her.

"I knew I brought it out of the house!"

"You did not," he says with a laugh. "You left it on the countertop, but I grabbed it for you lest you spend the entire afternoon in your tortured artist era."

"Oh, shut up!" she replies, pushing his arm. He grabs her hand, twisting it until he can press his lips against the back of her hand.

"Thanks for the artwork," he whispers. He drops her hand, then moves to stand up and brush the grass from his body. He picks up his sweater, squeezing it into his backpack while she packs up her stuff.

"Why did you let me draw on you if you had my book?" she asks.

"I'm art, baby." He smiles, throwing his arms out wide as he twists in front of her. He's utterly ridiculous, and possibly her favorite person in the entire world.

She wants to tell him he's always been art, but she settles with wrapping her arm around his waist instead. He loops his arm over her shoulder, then kisses her on the top of the head as they walk away.

CHAPTER TWENTY-FOUR

G ram's house looks much the same, the decor un-
changing for the entirety of Olivia's life. They're setting up in the living room, which leads through to the
kitchen. It's the perfect hosting house, and Olivia is sure
Grams bought it for that reason only. She finds the hook
behind the curtain pole and ties one end of the last piece
of bunting to it. She always thought it was extravagant, and
the quirkiest thing when she was younger—having an entire
hook drilled into the wall just to hang decorations with
ease—but now she gets it. Grams is always the host. It brings
her joy to host. So having something around that makes it
easier just makes sense.

She hands the other end of the bunting to Noah, and he
takes it with his free hand, the other resting against her lower
back like she might fall to her death from the three-step
ladder she's standing on. He doesn't move away until she's
safely back on the ground, and he sticks his tongue out at
her when she laughs at him.

"Laugh all you like, Lil," Noah states, hanging his end of the bunting up on the other side of the room with ease. "But we all know rolling an ankle means you'll never be able to walk comfortably for the rest of your life."

"Okay, dramatic."

"Don't blame me," he replies, holding his hands up. "Blame evolution and the fact that ankles are begging to be useless."

"Uh-huh." She laughs. She grabs some plates from the kitchen cabinet, placing them in a high stack on the kitchen side. The food will be placed out later. Grams always has her summer party catered, and Olivia remembers sitting on the couch with her plate full of food and a book. It's a weird memory; she can't tell if it's happy or not. She loves being around Grams and the Grants. She even liked Noah at these events, mainly. Sometimes he was annoying, but that wasn't his fault, not really. But she always spent the entire time tense, waiting to see if her parents were going to turn up. They always did, but they were never there for her, which made sense because it was not her party. But they did turn up for Grams, and for their appearances.

Every year, they'd turn up with a gift in hand, even though Grams asked for donations to charities only, and they'd be oh so happy to spend the day with family and close friends. It would bring a smile to Olivia's face, because she missed them. She always missed them. But when she got older, she stopped watching the door like a hawk because it reminded her that they'd always be here for this, but for her birthday, which is barely two weeks away, they suddenly had things to do that they couldn't get out of. They suddenly didn't appear with gifts and stories of their adventures to new places.

Suddenly, family meant nothing.

"You doing okay there, honey?" Grams asks, her hand shaking slightly as she holds on to the kitchen counter. She leans her walking stick next to her, and Olivia is sure she's a couple of inches shorter than the last time she saw her.

"Yeah," she replies with a smile. "How are you? Excited to see everyone?"

"Lord, I see them all at church. I'm only here for the food."

"I'm sure." Liv laughs. She's comfortable here. She's always been comfortable here, but there's an ache at the back of her throat. Grams looks tired and weary, her hair whiter than before, and Olivia has missed three years because she was too tied up in her grief to get on the train for people that truly cared about her.

"It's nice being back," Liv says, taking a deep breath. "Uhm . . ."

"Oh, don't you even worry about it, honey," Grams says, waving her off. "I was in college once, and I used to despise having to come home."

"It wasn't—I love being here. I love coming here," she says, her voice desperate as she tries to find the words she wants, the words she needs.

"I used to despise being at home," Grams repeats, placing her hand over Liv's, "and I had half-decent parents."

Liv shakes out a laugh, blinking back tears as she does. Grams has never been one to hide her feelings about people. She'd never call anyone out on the street, but if they didn't get a Christmas card, well . . .

"I still should have come back for this. For you," she whispers.

"Oh, honey." Grams laughs, pulling her into a hug. Olivia has to bend down, but she doesn't mind the effort. "I'm so glad you went away and did your own thing. We've been nothing but proud of you. But I am glad you're back, even if it's only for right now."

"Yeah?" Liv sniffs, holding on to the hug a beat longer than she normally would.

"Yes. Noah has been dragging himself around like a kicked puppy without you."

"He has not," Liv says with a laugh, letting go when Grams pulls back.

"Honey, you're the last one to see it," Grams says, with a look in her eye Liv would be foolish to miss. "But you're the only one who needs to see it, so being the last is okay."

Grams grabs her walking stick and winks at her, then walks away slower than the speed of moss, chuckling as she goes.

"You just drop a bombshell like that and then leave?" Liv calls after her.

She does, in fact, drop the bombshell and then just leave. So Liv spends the next half an hour blowing up balloons with her pump and tying them with a little too much force. Only four pop, so she's taking that as a win.

It's not as though she thought Noah would actually throw a parade the day she left. She certainly wasn't happy about him not being around anymore. She's even allowing herself to think that maybe, possibly, he might like her right now. He might be getting suckered into the fake-dating routine, just like she is. He might fall asleep thinking about her, as she does with him.

But she's never thought about him liking her *before*. She's never thought about him being obvious about it around other people. It's possible, of course, that Grams is delusional and she just wants Noah to like Olivia because Grams likes her so much. It could also be because adults always think boys like girls when they pick on them, and yes, Olivia probably picked on Noah more than he did with her, but adults see what they want to see.

"Guess what," Noah says, sliding across the kitchen floor in his socks. He hits the counter with a small thud and pouts as he rubs his hip. Olivia thinks she might be in love with him. She shoves it back down her throat and raises her eyebrows instead, lest the admission slips out onto the side with the plates.

"Your parents aren't coming. Well—" Olivia barely hears the rest. The anxiety leaves her in waves, the fear of having to watch the door for their arrival no longer necessary.

"Grams didn't invite them."

"She didn't?" Liv asks.

"Nah. She said she always used to because you were 'a baby,' but now she wants you to be happy, so . . ." He shrugs.

"Oh," she whispers.

"Unless you wanted to see them?" Noah panics. "I can go call them right now and—"

"Noah." She laughs, then says, "It's alright. It's better this way."

He gives her a look but ultimately lets it slide. She's not lying; it is better this way. It doesn't stop the ache in her chest, though, at the thought that now they have nothing to be here for, she might never see them again.

But she's not thinking about that, not tonight. Tonight she's going to enjoy the party. Mainly because Noah is close and she hasn't shouted firetruck at him for a good couple of days. The things that used to annoy her somehow morphed into the things that make her smile. The way he's always next to her—she likes feeling the heat from his body. The way he looks at her when he says a joke to check if she's laughing too. She thinks with him and the absence of her parents, she might actually enjoy tonight the way she always wanted.

CHAPTER
TWENTY-FIVE

O h, for the love of all things holy, how the fuck is Brendan here? He doesn't even live in this city. He doesn't have friends here, so how is he at this family party she barely wanted to be at, looking like a class-A prick?

"Ugh, my ex is here," Olivia grumbles before she can stop herself. She leans against the kitchen counter, wondering how gross it would be to ask Noah to pretend to be her boyfriend even if they're in front of his family. Technically, she is his girlfriend for random nights, but they've never spoken about *him* being *her* fake boyfriend, especially not when she called him out on being a big embarrassment when he first asked her. Besides, she's not sure she wants to be closer to him when she doesn't need to be, because it makes her head feel funny and Grams's words are rolling around her brain like a pinball machine. She's not even all that sure she wants it to be fake.

"What ex?" Noah asks, his brows furrowed. He looks uncharacteristically angry, and Liv isn't sure why. He is the person she tells the most to, but she still doesn't tell him everything—and he is definitely not aware of the former. Still, he moves to stand closer to her, and the muscles in his forearms flex as he crushes his beer can and throws it in the trash.

She sighs, scooching ever closer to Noah, if only to hide behind him. "Brendan."

"Oh no. Want me to beat him up?" Noah asks, letting out a strained laugh as his arm rests against hers.

"Shut up," Liv groans, running her forefinger over the tab of her drink. "He's a tool, but I should have known that when I agreed to go out with him."

"You don't strike me as the type to go out with tools," he replies, looking at her in a way she can't place. It makes her feel uncomfortable in a not-entirely-uncomfortable way.

"Well," she says, swallowing around a forced laugh, "I agreed to go out with you, so—"

"Ouch!" He smiles, his hand against his chest. She smiles back, but it fades as quickly as it came.

"I didn't know he was a tool," she whispers. It's not something she's happy about. She always prided herself on figuring people out, but she's truly never been good at it.

"Well, people can be deceiving," he replies. He looks at her then, his eyes flashing with nerves, but she's not sure what about. He leans in, and her heart thumps in her chest. Does she want to kiss him, or does she want him to kiss her?

Either way, it doesn't matter—he pulls back with a smirk, taking her drink as he goes.

"Yeah." She laughs. "You're still an asshole, though."

"You're so mean to me, Oli." Noah laughs with her, knocking her shoulder lightly. She looks up at him, and it always takes her by surprise when he's looking right at her, like he didn't just say her name—she forgets the rules of basic interaction whenever she can smell his cologne.

She kind of wants to hold his hand or lean her head against his shoulder, but she doesn't. She just looks at him for a few seconds.

"You're really beautiful," he says. Her eyes widen as she almost snaps her neck clean off so she can avoid looking at his face. She doesn't want to see when he turns from serious to playful and tells her he was only kidding. She certainly wants to avoid letting him see the blush that creeps across her cheeks.

"Shut up," she grumbles.

"Shan't." He laughs. She's about to lean against him, to see if he'll move his arm to rest behind her, when she watches Brendan walk over, a smug smile across his face. Their breakup wasn't exactly amicable.

"Oh, come on," she whispers, moving a step closer to Noah. He looks at her, then at Brendan, and back to her.

"Liv," Brendan says, cocky as anything. She smiles at him. No one would know it was fake if they looked over, but by his snort, she thinks Noah can tell.

"Only her friends call her Liv," Noah replies, a small smirk on his face that Brendan ignores.

"I'm Brendan," he says to Noah, holding his glass up in cheers as though Noah should know who he is. He does, technically, but still.

"Brendan? Baby," Noah says, sickly sweet as he turns to face her. "You didn't tell me about Brendan?"

"There's not much to tell," she grumbles. She's all for keeping the peace and being overly polite if she needs to be, but Brendan made her best friend cry by continuously calling her by her deadname, and for what? So she lets the passive aggressiveness slip out as Noah wraps his arm around her shoulder.

"This is Noah," she says, sipping her drink.

"Noah? Noah the one you were always desperately trying to avoid coming home to?" Brendan scoffs, and Liv tenses under Noah's arm. It's no shock that they didn't get on, but she feels bad all the same.

"She only hates me because I saw her naked as a baby," Noah jokes. Liv groans as she leans her forehead against Noah's neck. He's so annoying, but she finds herself laughing all the same. Her lips brush against his pulse, and she's no doctor, but she thinks his heart is beating too fast.

197

"Well, I saw her naked when I bent her over last term," Brendan says with a forced laugh.

"Fucking hell, Brendan," Liv whispers, and she can feel the embarrassment rolling off her in waves—probably going to coat Noah in a venomous green tinge.

"Well, I'll see you around." Brendan smirks, looking first at Noah, then he turns to Liv. "See you later tonight, hopefully."

"Not in your wildest dreams," she replies. She's furious. She's humiliated and she wants to leave. She wants to shout at him and tell him he was never good enough for her and that his views on people who are different from him are hideous and he's disgusting, but she can't. Because then she's the angry one, then she's the one who can't control her temper. And she's more than the angry Black girl stereotype. So she doesn't say anything.

"Yeah," Noah replies, holding his hand out. Brendan rolls his eyes but makes a big show of slapping his hand in Noah's, and if she weren't dying of embarrassment at the dick-measuring contest, she'd love the way Brendan's brows furrow when Noah squeezes his hand. He pulls Brendan's arm close to him, jolting him forward a few steps.

"If you ever speak to Liv like that again," Noah says, deathly calm, "I'll tear your fucking arm off."

Olivia walks away as Brendan shakes his hand out, probably trying to get the feeling back into it. Liv can defend herself. She knows Noah knows that. But she's unsure if he knows how desperately she's always wanted someone to have her back. For someone to stand up for her when she was in the seventh grade and say, actually, no, she can't stay at home by herself, her parents need to look after her. To defend her in college when a girl told her that her hair wasn't tidy enough for the first day of her internship and that she should straighten it from now on. To defend her when she can't defend herself because society has decided if she ever speaks beyond a polite tone, she's the aggressor simply because her skin is darker than theirs.

But she struggles with asking to be helped because there's never anyone there to help her. Sure, Noah pushed Luke over in the third grade when he called Liv a cruel name. And yeah, he always had her on his debate team so he could back her up when she said a perfectly valid statement, she just happened to have braids in that day which meant she was easily picked on.

She knows Noah would have her back if she let him. But she's humiliated, and she can't ask him for anything in case he says no and she loses the only person who's ever been there for her.

So she stands in the light rain just outside the back door, and for the first time she wishes she smoked because at least then she'd have something to do, somewhere to expel the pent-up frustration. But as she flicks her fingers, the door bursts open and she thinks she'll hit Brendan if he's followed her out here.

"Oli," Noah shouts, looking out into the garden. His face swivels frantically as he tries to find her, as if they're not safe in a suburban garden in the middle of a cul-de-sac.

"Oliv—"

"Yes?" He spins, looking at her like she's the only thing he needs to see right now, and it's distracting and over the top and everything she wants. "What—"

His lips are on hers before she can say anything, the softness of his lips making up for the force with which he pulled her to him. She should say something, probably, but she threads her hand through his hair to pull him closer, so she guesses she doesn't really have anything else to add.

The kiss slows down, but it does nothing to lessen the fireworks in her chest, the tingles at the base of her spine, or the way she needs to break away for air.

He pulls back as she does, his brows furrowed as he looks anywhere but at her. There's a time when she would have thought he'd regretted his actions, that maybe it was just a knee-jerk reaction and actually he didn't want to kiss her at all.

But there's no one in the world she knows as well as she knows Noah. So she knows he's nervous in the same way she is, and he's brought this as far as he can without her. So, she leans back in, watching his eyes soften as she does. Her lips touch his once, twice, three times before his hands pull her flush against him again.

"I don't need defending," she says, her tongue in his mouth before he can reply.

"I know," he gasps when she pulls back for air. "I'm going to defend you anyway."

"Dork," she breathes, her chest heaving. She wants to kiss him again. She thinks she might always want to kiss him. But the back door opens, and she tries to step back. He doesn't let her go that far.

"I've always got your back," he says, pressing his lips to her nose as she smiles at him.

"Yeah?"

"Yeah," he whispers, pulling her into a hug. "Always."

CHAPTER TWENTY-SIX

N oah convinces her to go back inside, and she lets him. She'd let him do whatever he wanted, probably.

He grabs her a snack that she lets sit on the plate next to her. She doesn't feel hungry, but she does feel safe when Noah tucks her hair behind her ear, looking at her like maybe, if she wished hard enough, he might like her back and it won't be for show.

"Noah!" someone calls, breaking their silent staring contest. She would have won either way; she loves looking at him.

"Oh God," he groans, his hand still against her neck. "Not Mrs. Laudrey."

"You've got to save your dad from her," Olivia says with a laugh. Mrs. Laudrey is an eighty-year-old woman who has lived next to Grams longer than Olivia and Noah have been alive. Her husband sadly passed about ten years ago, and ever since, she's called Joe when something needs to be done, and he goes, because of course he does. Now whenever there's an event, she always wants to dance because she and her husband used to go to classes together. It was soft and sweet and everything Liv used to smile about when she was at these parties. But now he's gone and Joe used to dance in college, so Mrs Laudrey never lets him out of her sight. Joe is the nicest man alive so he dances with her, but still, he needs a break every now and then.

"Mm-hmm." Noah laughs. He kisses her on the forehead before he says, "Just know that even though we'll dance and I'll do such a convincing job of being her much younger husband—"

"Sure, sure." Liv laughs, nodding at him as his smile settles into something familiar.

"You're still my favorite girl here."

"Oh, I am, am I?" she asks, her smile splitting her face in half without her permission.

He leans closer, his nose brushing hers before he turns to whisper in her ear.

"You're my favorite everywhere."

"Go dance with Carol before she comes over here," Liv replies, pressing her lips to his palm as he moves away.

No, this party has never been her favorite, but her parents aren't around, and Joe walks over to top her drink up with some nonalcoholic punch because he refuses to believe she's not still thirteen.

"Thanks," she replies as he leans against the counter next to her.

"Thank *you*," he stresses. "I thought for sure I was going to perish while doing the box step. I don't see why we have to have these parties every year." He huffs, then stuffs some grapes into his mouth.

"You don't like dancing with Mrs. Laudrey?" Olivia asks, stifling a smile as he scowls at her.

"Ugh." He laughs. "Only as much as you'd like to dance with Noah."

Olivia swallows, looking around the room instead of at Joe. Joe calls her out at the best of times, and he'd definitely be able to figure out she thinks she might maybe like him a lot. He'll almost certainly start cheering if he looks at her and realizes she's in love with Noah.

"*Oh . . .*"

"Shh." Liv laughs, still refusing to look at him.

"You finally caught up, huh?"

"What?" Olivia's head snaps up to look at him.

He's giving her a look, and she understands what he's saying even if she pretends she doesn't, because Noah has never been one to shy away from his feelings, and he's been obvious with his pursuit, even if she thought it was supposed to be fake at the start.

"He'd never tell you because he wouldn't want you to think less of him," Joe says. "He spent all his life with you hating him, and I don't think he could bear to go back to that—not now he knows you better. Not that I'm sure there was ever a time you two weren't in each other's pockets."

"I don't think I could think badly of him," Olivia whispers. "I've never hated him."

"I know that." Joe shrugs. "But I'm not a teenage boy with a crush on the girl next door."

He smiles at her, and then walks away as if he hasn't just left a bomb in her chest. As if she's supposed to just deal with this information that has been floating around her head but she's been too terrified to actually think about.

No, she doesn't hate Noah. Now when she hears him singing in the shower, she wants to be there with him instead of growling at the wall. Now when he's pacing too loudly in his room, she wants to ask him what's wrong instead of telling him to shut up. Now she wants him to tell her anything and everything he might want.

Olivia looks at the hoards of people in the house, the ones she's known since she was a baby, and none of them hold any weight for her (well, other than Helen, Joe, Grams and Murphy if he managed to make the trip). Her eyes fly over them all in her pursuit to find the only person she cares about. She's not sure if she has the courage to tell him that right now, but she wants to see him all the same.

But as her eyes sweep over people, her breath catches in her throat.

"Oh, no," she whispers. It's not who she wants to see right now, because she's how she always is when she sees them—alone. She's not even seeing them for a good reason. It's her birthday in a matter of days, and she knows they won't even stay in town for that.

It's always the same, and the worst thing in the world to her—they're not even here for her.

They walk over anyway, hugging people as they do, smiles plastered to their faces that Liv can't even tell if they're fake or not.

"Livi!"

"Hi, Mom. Hi, Dad."

CHAPTER TWENTY-SEVEN

Her mom's arm is loose around Olivia's shoulder as she talks to Bridget from three doors down. She tells her how proud she is that Livi finished college with such great grades (Olivia isn't sure they even know what course she did). She tells them all how excited she is for "whatever Livi wants to do next." It's supposed to sound supportive, all "of course we'd support her, no matter what," and everyone smiles and acts like her parents are the best thing since sliced bread.

She's the only one around that knows they're only saying that because they have no idea what she wants to do. She'd be surprised if they even knew she wanted to be a graphic designer, that she majored in English but took a minor in graphics. They have no idea that she's wavering between two jobs—the main issue being she doesn't want to be here because it reminds her of them.

Her mom looks the same. Her hair is different, but her hair changed week to week anyway. The last time Olivia saw her, her mom had braids, and today her hair is straightened. That's the main difference, she thinks—she can't really remember.

Her father looks different. More tired. Maybe a little thinner. She doesn't think he's sick, maybe just overworked. She doesn't know how to ask, and she doesn't know if they'll tell her the truth either way. Maybe the next time she sees them at a party they didn't tell her they were going to, he won't be there at all. Maybe he'll die and she won't know until she sees Grace from floor two at the grocery store, and she'll ask her why she wasn't at the funeral.

She feels the panic start in the base of her feet. It travels slowly through her body, threatening to choke her as they ask her how she's feeling and if she got sugar from the store as they asked. As if they saw her this morning. As if she hasn't aged in front of their very eyes. As if they give a shit about her.

She swallows, blinking rapidly as she wills her breathing to calm down. No one notices, of course—she can only see the back of her mother's head as she talks about her like she's not right there. Liv wants to tell her she's not allowed to call her Livi because her name is Olivia, and the only people she lets give her a nickname are the people that love her. (She doesn't.) Liv wonders if she's wearing her wedding ring, if she and her father are even still together. They turned up together, but they've never done anything that wasn't to keep up appearances.

Olivia can't ask them that right now. She can't ask them if they're in love and happy, or if maybe they regret having a child, or if maybe, just maybe, they miss her too. She can't tell them that she missed them but the space in her heart that she left for them is slowly being filled with other things. Noah owns more of her heart than they ever have, but she can't tell them that—they don't deserve to know that. She can't tell them anything, because she can barely breathe. There's a possibility she might choke to death right behind them, with her arm reaching out for them, but they won't even notice she's there. A fitting portrayal, she thinks, for how their lives have been.

"Take my hand," Noah whispers, his lips lightly against her shoulder.

She does, and before she knows it, she's being whisked through the crowd. She thinks she hears someone say her name, but she doesn't know who—and it's not Noah, so she doesn't really care.

The lights are a blur, and she's not sure of anything at all until the chilly air hits her exposed arms. It's only for a moment because Noah places his sweater over her shoulders. She looks up at him, his eyes tracking her every moment as he stands in front of her. Olivia doesn't like to be touched by anyone when she feels overwhelmed. She knows Noah knows that, but he doesn't know that he's not included in everyone else. It's everyone else, and then there's him.

Her vision settles slightly. The edge of her sight remains fuzzy, but she can see Noah. The concern that snakes across his face, the worry folding into the crease between his eyebrows. So, she feels a sense of calm anyway, even if the sparks in her brain are refusing to lessen.

"I'm okay," she whispers. It's all she can do. It's all she can say. But it's enough to get him to move. His hand works its way behind her neck, and he pulls himself closer until her forehead is resting against his chest.

"You're okay," he repeats, though she's not sure it's for her.

Before she knows it, she's sliding into a booth at their favorite pizza place. She has to shuffle in because she's in a dress and the tacky material on the benches sticks to her skin the second the temperature hits double digits.

Olivia doesn't say much at all. Noah takes control of ordering food and drinks. She's not hungry, even if she didn't eat at the party, but the quiet of the pizzeria soothes her heart, even if she still needs to trace the pattern on the edge of the napkin just to calm down. Whenever she panics, she

THE LAST GOOD THING

just needs a quiet place. Not too quiet, because then she'll be able to hear the blood pulsing too fast in her ears and she'll be able to hear her own thoughts and she doesn't want those at the best of times.

It starts raining harder, and she turns her head to watch the raindrops running down the window. She likes to pick one and follow it to see if it's going to beat all the other raindrops to the end.

"Mine won," Noah says, pulling her out of her head as she spins to face him.

"What?" she asks, her eyes widening as she sees the pizzas on the table. They're still steaming, the vegetables on Noah's pizza chargrilled to perfection, as they always are here.

"My raindrop—Terry—he won the race." He shrugs.

"He did not." Olivia pouts. She reaches for a piece of pizza she's not sure she wants.

"Don't be jealous, baby," he replies, taking a large bite of his own slice. He widens his eyes at the pizza in her hand, and she knows he's challenging her to eat it. He's ridiculous, but she loves him, so she takes an exaggerated bite, even if it's only to make him smile. (And when it works, she feels as though she could slay dragons.)

She swallows and takes a sip of her water before she almost coughs it back up through laughter as she remembers the words Noah said. At least something funny happened tonight.

"What?" Noah asks, smiling at her.

"I can't believe you told Brendan you'd tear his arm off."

"I would, too!" Noah laughs with her, his eyes crinkling at the edges. He takes a slice of her pizza, but she doesn't mind. She likes to share with him.

"You wouldn't hurt a fly," she replies, resting her head in her palm.

"I would for you." He shrugs. "I wouldn't like it, but I'd do it anyway."

"Yeah?"

"Yeah." He smiles. "Are you feeling any better?"

"Mm-hmm."

"Enough to eat a whole slice?" he asks, pushing the pan toward her. She pouts, but he scrunches his eyes closed before he sees it.

"Not gonna work," he replies, and she leans back against the bench. She likes looking at Noah, but she wishes he was here. On her side. Maybe in a moment, she'll move. Maybe she'll be the brave one. For now, she takes another bite of pizza.

"How are you feeling, really?" Noah asks, reaching for her fingers. She sighs, the weight of the evening hitting her full force as Noah rubs his thumb over the back of her hand. It's not even that she's missed her parents, she doesn't think. It's not even that they probably haven't noticed she's gone.

"I just—my dad looks sick."

"Is he?" Noah asks, his head cocked to the side.

"I don't know," she whispers. It settles in her chest. The realization that that's why she's so upset. There's a chance he is sick and she's missed years of him not being sick. There's nothing she could have done, not really—she knows that somewhere under the layers of regret. Could she have messaged them more in college? Could she have told them she wanted to spend time with them when she was at home? Probably.

Does she think it would have made a difference?

The answer is too hard to let into her mind.

"Ah."

"You see," she mumbles.

"I see," he says. He rubs his thumb over her knuckles, but it isn't enough. So she shuffles out of the booth, keeping his hand in hers as she crawls into his side.

"Hi." She leans against him, and he immediately wraps his arm around her shoulders.

"Hi, baby," he replies, then says, "Do you wanna stay here, or do you wanna go home?"

"Can I stay at yours tonight?" she asks, playing with his fingers. She's pretty sure her parents won't stay at their apartment tonight and they'll be out of town by tomorrow, but still. She doesn't want to risk it.

"You can stay forever."

CHAPTER
TWENTY-EIGHT

In the end, Olivia eats three slices of pizza, and Noah eats the rest. It's how pretty much all of their meals go. She doesn't mind.

On the way back to his place, they walk along the promenade. It's different at nighttime. It's peaceful, like it was built just for them. Their fingers are linked loosely, and she's about to change that by wrapping her hands around his arm, but he pulls them into a slight jog up to their place on the wall.

"Sit here and look pretty," he says, placing her softly on their spot. His thumbs rub against her ribcage as she attempts to get her heart to slow down. She's not sure she minds that he can probably hear it when he looks at her like that.

He pulls back, winking at her as he turns and runs.

"Noah!"

"Trust me!" he shouts back, slowing to a jog as he comes face to face with a tree. She watches as he fiddles around, and she can't stop from giggling.

Whenever Olivia is out here, she spends her time watching the light dance on the waves. But tonight, she's content to watch Noah. She wishes she had her sketchbook so she could take some doodles of him in the ridiculous positions he's in trying to get *something* to stand up. She laughs when he throws his hands in the air.

"Stop laughing at me!" he says, spinning around to face her, and obviously, his ridiculous pout makes her laugh harder, but he seems content with his work as he jogs back over to her.

"What are you doing?" she asks, pulling him closer to her the second she's able to.

"We need to recreate our summer photo, Ol. Mom will love it."

"You're always sitting next to me," she says, patting the wall next to her.

"But I can't do this from there," he whispers, pulling her into a kiss. It's slow and deep, and it forces a shiver up her spine. She reaches for him, her hand deep in his hair, and he licks his tongue into her mouth. There's a pull deep in her stomach, something twisting and flipping as he bites at her lip—all it makes her want to do is pull him closer, but she can't. Even with the extra adrenaline from the kiss, she's not strong enough. All too soon, the kiss comes to a natural end, and if they were anywhere other than a public walkway, she might do something about it, but for right now, she's content to rest her forehead against his as she wills her breathing to level out.

"I need—" Noah pants, his voice shot as he grips her hips. "I need to get my phone before it's stolen by a raccoon."

"You're the most ridiculous person I know," she whispers in response. She wants to tell him she loves him anyway, but she watches him race to the tree and back instead.

Noah shows her the photos, the dark night sky lit up with millions of stars. It's not exactly like the originals because they were always taken during the day, the sky brighter than tonight, but it was always her favorite memory. She's not sure it is now, not with how this summer is going.

"Why are you so pretty all the time?" he asks, flipping through the photos that are surely not going to be shown to his mother. They'll have to figure something else out for her birthday.

"You can't even see me in this," she replies. But he pulls up a photo where they are both smiling at each other. They're a little too close for it to be friendly, but she gathers everyone else already knows she's in love with him, so what's the use in hiding it?

"You're always pretty," he mutters, sliding his phone back into his pocket. He walks in front of her slightly and she wonders what he's playing at, but he doesn't make her wait long.

"Noah!" she squeals as he hoists her onto his back, his hands heavy under her thighs.

"Let's go home."

She's never sure how comfortable it actually is to give someone a piggyback, but she can hook her chin over his shoulder, so she'll let him carry her until his knees give in. All she really knows is that she wants all of her good days to be with him.

And all of her bad days too.

CHAPTER
TWENTY-NINE

N oah gives her some of his pajamas, scoffing that he's going to have to buy more because he already knows she's going to take them home, and she simply does not correct him. He's gone to grab her a drink as she makes herself comfy in his bed. She's slept over here so many times before that it shouldn't feel strange, but as she looks around at the changes that have happened in the last four years, she realizes it's not the same at all.

There are still photos of them from high school in frames on the shelves on the wall. There's still a bookcase that looks like it wants to buckle under the weight of his soccer trophies and books Liv had given him. The walls are still a light blue, but there's something else. The cologne in the air and the college sweatshirt hanging on the back of his door.

He comes barreling in moments later, and she rolls her eyes because it's late and he's definitely going to get a letter from Mrs. Belmont downstairs.

"You're a Neanderthal." She laughs as she pulls his duvet up to her chin. It smells like him, and a little like home.

He throws his post on his bedside table, the energy radiating off him enough to get her worried that maybe he's hurt, or maybe someone else is hurt, because he's positively manic. It's a stark contrast to how he left this room mere seconds ago.

"What's wrong?" she asks, her eyes tracking over his face. She climbs out of his bed, his T-shirt barely covering her bum, but she doesn't care. Maybe it's Helen. Maybe Joe fell.

"I got in," he breathes, his chest heaving with the effort to keep his voice level. There's a letter shaking in his hand, and she can barely process what he's saying.

"What?"

"Um, to—" He swallows and takes a deep breath. "To the residency program. I got in."

"Oh my God!"

"I know," he whispers, blinking rapidly.

"Noah!" She squeals and throws her arms around his neck. He hugs her back, but she can feel his palms trembling against her shoulder blades.

"Hey," she says, pulling away slightly. His eyes track over her face, and she knows he's been waiting for this for weeks, but she thought he'd be happier about it. "Let's sit," Olivia suggests. She pulls the duvet back, getting him to sit on the sheets with his back against the headboard. She sits facing him.

"Hey," she repeats, and he flicks his gaze to her. "Talk to me."

"I don't think I can do it."

"Okay . . ." She knows Noah doesn't do well with praise he doesn't think he deserves, even though he does deserve it, and she's not a doctor, but she can help him now. "Why not?"

"I don't know," he says, pulling her closer with his hand on her ankle. "I'd be in charge of saving children. What if—"

"Hey," she whispers, holding his face with her hands. "Hey."

"Hi, baby."

"It's okay to be nervous, but you're not going to be alone, and you—Noah." She laughs as he looks at her. "You've trained for this. You were born to do this. Of course you should do it."

He breathes out, closing his eyes as he leans his head against the headboard.

"You're right. You're always right." He smiles. "I just—I had to ask you because, well, your opinion matters more to me than anyone's."

She blinks rapidly, trying to remember he's asking her serious questions, but her heart is thumping to get out of her chest at the fact that he cares about what she thinks.

"You didn't say that when I told you not to cut your hair in eighth grade," she says. It's not something she ever gave much thought about at the time—not really, it was more a passing question around the dinner table—but it does what it's supposed to do. It makes him laugh.

"You're so—" He laughs, pulling her into a hug. It's awkward until she throws her leg over his waist. Now her knees aren't clumped together next to his hip.

"It's different now," he whispers, his hands running up her thighs. "You really think I can do it?"

"I think you could do anything," she replies truthfully. "But I think the children are lucky you chose medicine."

"Yeah?"

"Yeah. You're so good. You're going to be so fucking good."

He blinks, and then a smile blooms on his face and he's the most beautiful thing she's ever seen.

"You think so?"

"I know so," she replies, pressing her lips to his nose. "Doctor Grant sounds so good on you."

His grip tightens on her leg as his eyes darken. It wasn't what she meant, but she's not mad at the outcome.

"Let it be known," he says, his voice low as she moves forward a tad, "you can call me that whenever you want."

"I'll bear that in mind," she replies, her eyes closing as she brings her lips to his. He tastes like mint and a little like happiness.

CHAPTER THIRTY

O livia walks down the street with people staring at her. She's used to it, so it doesn't phase her. Sometimes it's because she's the only Black person in the vicinity. Sometimes it's because her hair looks fabulous. Sometimes it's because she's carrying two large helium balloons.

Today is the latter (and to be fair, her hair looks great too).

She's going to meet Helen at Frankie's for Noah's surprise lunch. It's nothing too fancy, just her, Helen, Joe, Grams, and Noah (if Joe manages to get him there on time). There's a part of her that feels guilty she hasn't told any of them about the job offer sitting in the inbox of her phone. It's not because she doesn't want to tell them, or that she wants to avoid a celebration lunch she knows they'll throw her. She just doesn't want to get their hopes up that she might stay—only to leave.

"Hey." She smiles as she walks into the cafe. Helen is scattering some confetti on the table, and Grams is definitely on her second mimosa already. Liv leans in to hug Helen and

Grams first, without thinking about it. It's just part of their routine now.

There's also a part of her that thinks it would be different this time around. She could move four hours away and she wouldn't need to actually leave them. She wouldn't need to disappear altogether. She could take the train for Grams's party, and Noah could drive up to visit her on the weekends or whatever days worked with his residency.

Olivia ties the balloons to the back of Noah's chair. It's obvious it's his place because it has cards and an obnoxiously large badge. Helen waves her hands to get her attention just as she sees Joe and Noah walking past the large windows of the café. They're not looking in, but Liv knows it's only for show. Joe is the worst secret keeper—Noah is going to have known since this morning, maybe even last night.

Either way, he acts surprised when he walks in. His eyebrows shoot up, and his smile takes her breath away. Helen runs around to hug him, swinging slightly in the middle of the floor. There's a part of her that would have ached for this reaction from her parents, about anything really, but she can't find any jealousy in her body, not today.

Noah walks over and pulls her into a tight hug. She breathes him in like she didn't see him just yesterday morning. She holds on to him like she didn't wake up with him barely twenty-four hours ago.

"Hey," she says.

"Hi, baby," he whispers.

"Did you know?" she asks, lingering in the hug a beat too long if the look on Grams's face is anything to go by. She pulls back as he smiles lightly.

"Of course." Noah pulls her chair out for her, and she sits down, pulling her phone out so she can capture him opening his cards. The balloons float above his head, and the sunlight bathes him in a golden glow. She changes her phone background.

As lunch progresses from sandwiches to desserts and the talk of a walk down to the seafront, Olivia realizes something. There's another part of her, a part she tries not to look at, that says she doesn't want to leave here at all. That she's already tried that. She left, and now she's back and somehow everything is better than ever. There's a part of her heart that would be left here either way, whether she wanted to leave it or not. There's a part of her that's no longer entirely hers. She's given it away over shared ice creams and walks along the promenade. She's handed it over every time he asked for her hand. Every time he pressed his lips to hers. She's given it to him, and she didn't even realize it.

She spent her entire life relying on herself only, on keeping her heart locked away, and she's handed it to Noah without even thinking about it.

"Hey," Noah whispers as he steals a spoonful of her chocolate and hazelnut ice-cream.

"What's up, baby?" she whispers back.

"Do you want to go out with me tomorrow?" he asks, swallowing as he does.

"Sure," she replies easily. "What is it? And how do you have so many friends that throw parties every four seconds?"

He laughs, though it sounds strained. "It's not a party."

"No? What is it then?"

"Uh . . ." He rubs his lips together. "I thought we could go to that pottery place you were looking at a couple of weeks ago. I'll even get the matching saucer to the tiny mug if you want."

"Oh," she replies, smiling at him and trying to ignore Grams staring at her from behind Noah's shoulder. "Like a date?"

"Yeah," he breathes, then says, "Like a date."

She's given him her heart, and it's the best thing she's ever done.

CHAPTER
THIRTY-ONE

The door to her apartment closes behind them, and Noah places her bag on the hook. She drops his hand as she rushes to the toilet. She loves everything about summer, apart from the queues for the bathrooms.

She runs past a cardboard box on the floor and she thinks they're flowers, but she's not sure what for—she just recognizes the packaging.

"Can you open that?" she asks as she clicks the bathroom door closed. Olivia always thought it was weird that she could see herself while she was sitting on the toilet. The mirror in the bathroom touches the sink, all the way to the ceiling. But she doesn't mind now, fixing her hair as she sits down.

"Pretty!" Noah shouts. She hears a clinking of cupboard doors as he searches for a vase. Her mind barely lingers on who sent flowers and why, mainly focusing on what Noah would look like arranging flowers. She washes her hands, then checks her makeup in the mirror. It's mainly fine. She dabs the end of her nose with a tissue. She's always been an oil-slick mess, and suncream never helps.

She walks out, the light pink peonies still in the bud staring at her. So they're from Steph. Steph always sends peonies if she can. Olivia tries to get a look at the card, the front saying congratulations in bubble writing, and *oh.*

It's about the job. The job she got that she hasn't told Noah about. She hasn't spoken about it since their first dinner, so she'll be surprised if he remembers anything about it anyway.

"What's this?" Noah asks, the card from Steph in his hands. "Did you get the job?!"

"Yeah," she replies, feeling the guilt roll off her when he looks at her. It's a mixture of excitement and something else she tries to ignore. Something that looks like he's wondering why on earth she didn't tell him.

"Oli! That's amazing." He hugs her, and she hides her face against his shoulder so she doesn't have to think about how she should have told him weeks ago. He's going to ask her why she didn't tell him, and she doesn't have a good enough reason just yet.

"Thanks," she breathes.

"I'm so happy for you. That's—wow, that's both of them now, right?" he asks.

"Yeah," she replies, her lip caught between her teeth as he pulls back.

"They waited a while, sheesh," he says, widening his eyes as he places the card with the flowers.

"I found out a while ago."

"Oh. Oh, okay, that's—why didn't you tell me?" It's not unkind, but it gives her no movement at all. She wants to tell him the truth, but that means figuring out what she wants to do. The truth means telling him she loves him, and that was never the plan. The truth means telling him she wanted to leave, even though he was right here, and now she's not sure what she wants. The truth means telling him she wasn't supposed to fall in love with him but she never had a choice.

"When they said I'd gotten onto my residency," he says, his voice low, "you were the first person I wanted to tell."

The job decision has always been difficult because she never wanted to rely on her parents. And she was used to that. She knew that was what was making it so hard for her to decide. But now she's not so sure.

She can't tell if she wants to take the job at home despite her parents because Noah is here. She doesn't know if she's even allowed to factor him into the decision. She brought herself up watching strong women on screen and reading about them in books, and it's always the same. Don't take the job for a man—and she never would—but can she even include him in the pros and cons list?

She's always wanted to be a graphic designer. It's what she trained for. It's what she's good at. So ever since she applied for this position, she knew deep down she wanted it. The other offer is less money, it's less responsibility, it's barely even in her field, but at least it's not here. The only thing keeping her from her dream job was the reality of having to stay at home. It never had anything to do with him. But now Noah is here, exactly where he's always been, and she can't separate her heart from her mind.

So, she tells him half the truth.

"I knew you'd tell me to take the job."

"You don't want it?" he asks. It's a simple question, but it renders her speechless all the same.

"I—I would have to stay here."

"Do you want to leave?" he asks, swallowing thickly. He'd tell her to go if that's what she really wanted. He'd help her pack and he'd drive her wherever she needed to go, but he'll call her out on her bullshit as well, if he thinks she's leaving for the wrong reasons, and she's not sure she's ready for that yet.

"Not—I just—I don't want to live in this apartment, but I can't—I can't go anywhere else because I'm not a millionaire," she huffs.

"Why can't you stay here?"

She looks at him, the words unable to move past her throat.

"Don't make it harder for yourself just to spite them," Noah says when she doesn't respond. "I know you don't want to take anything from them, but housing is the absolute bare minimum that you can take."

"I just," she mutters, twisting her fingers together. "I don't want to be dependent on them." She doesn't want to be dependent on him, either. He'd never make her feel that way, and he'd never let her change so much about herself that she became dependent on him, but it scares her either way.

"You should be! You should have been."

"I just want to prove I can do it without them," she says.

"That's all you've ever done," Noah pleads. "You're the last good thing they ever did."

"Noah—"

"Oli," he says, his voice kind. "Will they even notice if you leave?"

"Jesus." She laughs, her hand against her chest. His question hurts, but he soothes it with his hand against hers.

"I'd notice. If you weren't around, I'd notice."

"Noah," she whispers.

"I get it. I get that you don't want to be reliant on them, but—"

"No, you don't, Noah." She sighs. "You've only ever had a loving family, okay? No one you love ever left you."

"You left."

"What?" she asks, feeling like the wind has been knocked out of her. She takes a step back, but she feels the wall behind her. She's trapped. The only way out is to talk to him.

"You left. You just—you were gone, like you didn't care at all that I was here."

"That's not—" She feels the lie crawl up her throat. "I just had to get away."

"You've been here my entire life." He laughs, but there's no humor in it. "And you left like it wasn't a big deal if I was in your life or not, and now you're back, and I'm not sure how to live without you—I'm not sure I ever want to."

Noah had always been here. He was the only thing that remained "here," even when she left. When she made it so she basically disappeared, Noah was there. He's always been there. He's never once let her down, but she can't have everything riding on one person, because when she inevitably fucks it up, she'll lose the only person in her life that's ever had her back.

She can't look at him, because if she looks at him, she'll definitely tell him things she shouldn't. Like *how she needs him* things. *He's her favorite thing* things. *She loves him* things.

"You were so used to acting like you didn't care if anyone was there for you that you missed what was right in front of you."

"What?" she asks, her eyes flicking across his face.

"It's always been you, Oli."

"We—we were kids," she whispers, blinking back the tears she knows are desperate to fall. She's never allowed herself to think about him wanting her when they were younger. About the possibility that maybe he loved her when he asked her how her weekend was. When he asked if she was going to come on his family's summer holiday. When he made sure her plate was full at every meal. She never let herself think about it because it would be too devastating if it wasn't true.

"It's always going to be you."

"Noah—"

"But you don't know how to ask for things, Liv. You don't—you just—you'd rather be lonely than admit you might need someone."

And she cries when she's stressed, so she changes tactics—anything to stop herself from crying right now, because he'll comfort her, and she'll let him.

"I know you're going to be a doctor, Noah, but I'm not someone you can fix," she stresses, balling her hands into fists.

"I'm not—what?" he asks, his mouth dropping slightly. "I know that, I don't—I don't want to fix you. You don't need to be fixed."

"I know," she states, but it's feeble at best. She was more convincing in her sixth-grade play, and she played a door.

"You don't need to be fixed," he repeats.

"I know that."

"*Olivia.*"

"I know," she mutters, even if she doesn't believe it. He takes a step forward, and she tries to take a step back, but the wall stops her movements as he gets ever closer. He lifts his hands once, twice, before he commits to resting them lightly against her hands. She lets him unwind her balled-up fingers, loosely connecting his with hers.

He looks at her like everything she's ever wanted. He looks at her like she's been thinking about when she's not even thinking.

She drops her gaze to their hands instead.

"Oli," he says, his hand lifting her chin back to him, and he's somehow closer than she expected and nowhere near close enough. She wants to let him love her. She wants to let him do whatever he wants with her. She wants this to not be fake.

But as she watches him swallow, she remembers everything she has to lose. She survived losing Brendan. She survived losing her parents. But she's not sure she'll survive losing Noah. At least this way she can keep him, even if it's at a distance.

"I loved you then, and I—"

"Firetruck," she whispers. She feels his shaky breath more than she hears it, and her heart hits the floor.

He looks devastated, and she understands why, but she can't get her mouth to move. To tell him that she wants to kiss him, that she wants him to be there for her, that she loves him. But she can't. She's spent too long dealing with relationships that fail. Where the people that are supposed to love her the most leave.

She figures it's not all that different now, because she watches as Noah walks away, the door closing behind him.

CHAPTER
THIRTY-TWO

O livia has felt heartbreak before. She's sure of it. Her heart hurts whenever she thinks of how her parents don't care about her. She was in pain when she broke up with Brendan.

But this is different. And it's unfair because she never even got to tell Noah out loud that she loved him. He has no idea how she feels about him. She has no way of knowing if it's something he would have liked to hear, or if he would have run for the hills.

She never wanted to admit to herself how she felt about Noah, because anytime she got close, she thought about how it would end. About how she might lose him.

But now she has let herself think about it, and it hurts like she thought it would.

All she's left with as she sits on her bed is an empty, sinking feeling, her chest caving in on itself as she wills herself not to cry. He's only next door, and a few weeks ago that would have been enough. It probably would have annoyed her if she managed to convince herself she wasn't in love with him for more than three seconds.

She hears movement in his bedroom, his footsteps as he walks toward his bed, and for a moment, she thinks he might come back. He might knock on her wall and climb through the fire escape like she didn't just crush his heart.

But then it stops, and she's left with silence—the same fucking silence back, and it's all she can do to not scream at the wall. It wouldn't be a surprise if Olivia's heart fell out of her chest. She wants it to. She wants it to splatter against the floor so she can see exactly where it hurts, so she can fix it—but she was never destined to be a doctor. The only person that could fix it is Noah. But it thumps in her chest all the same, taunting her that it still works, albeit slightly different than before.

She feels cold, heavy, as if she's been thrown into freezing water. Noah would tell her she was being dramatic, but he'd give her his hoody all the same. He'd probably wrap his hands around her feet and press his lips to her shins just to hear her laugh.

Maybe she got exactly what she wanted. A guy that she loves from a distance—because then at least he wouldn't leave. There's a stubborn lump in her throat that she can't swallow, and it hits her at that moment, as she leans back against the headboard, squeezing her eyes closed.

She only ever wanted him.

Olivia can't ask Helen about what to do with the hole in her chest because, well, she's Noah's mother. She can't ask Steph what to do because she'll tell her to just go and talk to him, but she wasn't there. She didn't see his face. She doesn't know Olivia has no idea how she would even go about it.

Besides, the only person she really wants to talk to is Noah, but she can't, and it's all her fault.

So, she does the only thing she can think of. She doesn't even care if it makes her feel bad; she can't feel any worse than she already does.

She texts her mom.

Liv: **Hey, just wondering how you were doing. Do you want to do something this weekend? It's been a while.**

She doesn't bother tossing her phone away, not because she hasn't come to terms with the fact that her mother won't reply, but mainly so she can reread texts she received from Noah back when she didn't feel like there was a truck running over her body.

She barely gets to last week before she's crying.

It's the last thing she remembers when she falls asleep.

Olivia wakes up with a rock in her chest and a lump in her throat. The first thing she does is check her phone. There's nothing from Noah, but she didn't expect there to be. She's not sure she deserves there to be.

She swallows around the lump in her throat, but it does nothing to dislodge it. It's heavy, dragging her heart down to her stomach as she blinks herself properly awake. She's not sure if she slept at all with the way the back of her eyes burn. She coughs into her arm, her throat feeling like it's been filled with barbed wire. She forgot to look at the time when she checked her phone, but the light blue sky suggests it's too early for her to be awake.

Still, the vague memory of texting her mom forces its way into her mind, slyly trying to edge out the pain and heartache associated with Noah's name. She still thinks about him anyway—she's always thinking about him.

Olivia grabs her phone, but of course, there's no response from her mom. She doesn't bother checking to see if her mom has read it.

She texts Steph instead.

Oli: **I really fucked things up.**

Stephhhhh (pretzel emoji): **did you fall in love with him?**

Oli: **Yes.**

Stephhhhh (pretzel emoji): **Just go and talk to him. Do not pass go, do not collect £200. Just go. And. Talk. To. Him.**

CHAPTER THIRTY-THREE

Helen invites her for dinner for her birthday, and despite what he said the other day, she knows Noah hasn't asked her to do so. Olivia used to like having her birthday a few days after Helen's because it was always an event. It lasted days, and the sole focus wasn't just on her, so no one questioned why Olivia was with them on her birthday instead of her own parents—it was always just what happened because their birthdays were close.

This year, she's not as excited. Helen's dinner isn't actually on her birthday this year, because she and Joe were out of town. So, it's the day before Olivia's. Usually, she doesn't care about her birthday anyway, so it wouldn't be an issue, but now her heart feels like it's been through a meat grinder, so she wants to stay at home and eat ice cream and she certainly doesn't want to see Noah. Well, she does want to see Noah, but she only wants to see him if she's figured out exactly what she wants to say to him.

What she'd really like is for him to crawl around in her mind, to find the thoughts she's too scared to share with herself but will gladly give over to him. What she wants is for him to figure out she's desperately in love with him but she's useless and doesn't know what to do with that information, even though she's ninety-seven percent sure he might like her back.

He might even love her. But she doesn't know how to let someone love her the way she knows he will. The thought terrifies her enough to sit on the sidelines and love him from a distance.

So, she wants to sit in bed in her pajamas and watch Bridget Jones's Diary and hopefully pass out before eight p.m.

But, for as much as she loves Noah, she loves Helen too.

So she knocks on their apartment door at six thirty, a bottle of wine and a record in hand. She's pushed her emotions so far down she's practically stepping on them. She can do one evening without letting her feelings bubble to the surface. She's great at that.

"Livi!" Helen greets her, pulling her into a hug.

"Hey! Happy birthday," she replies, trying not to hit her on the back with her gift bag.

"Oh, thank you, sweetheart."

Helen ushers her into the apartment. A small group of Helen's friends and family are gathered in the kitchen, and a few are seated in the living room. Noah sits against the windowsill, laughing at something his cousin Patrick said to him. Liv doesn't really know where to stand. She feels completely out of her depth. This is the first time she's ever been in this apartment without knowing how Noah would react. She almost misses the time she'd look over at him and he'd shout firetruck in her face.

But he hasn't seen her yet, so she swallows and gestures for Helen to open her gift, if only to bide some time before she takes her seat at the table.

"Oh, Livi," Helen cries. (She cries at most things, but Liv doesn't mind.) Olivia pulls her lip between her teeth as she smiles at her. Helen only ever deserves the best the world has to offer.

"Joe, look," she says, her voice watery as she wipes her eyes with the back of her hand. Liv hugs them both, feeling more settled as Joe immediately moves to put it on. Olivia doesn't look around the room because she knows her eyes will find Noah, and she's not sure how she'll react now that her emotions have already begun simmering to the surface. So much for her pep talk in her bedroom. Fucking useless.

The instruments start, and she feels her pulse in her ears. She smiles as Joe holds his hand out for Helen, the two slowly swaying, surrounded by their guests.

She doesn't mean to, but she looks around, just a little, to see who else is here. Of course, as she hears the slow, deep voice of Elvis singing "Can't Help Falling In Love," her gaze falls on Noah.

He's already looking at her.

She turns away, takes a deep breath, and tries to steady her hands. The look is familiar and brand new all at the same time. She's not sure how someone can feel like home to her when she's not even sure how to talk to them. It's a torturous feeling she tries to ignore, though it claws at her throat all the same.

"Liv!" Patrick shouts. He's only twelve, so she forgives him for shouting over the low volume of the music. He cringes, his shoulders nearly hitting his ears as his brother, Alex, hits him in the arm.

"Hey, Pat," Liv replies, walking over. She hugs him because he's cute and she remembers him being shy when she used to babysit him in the summer. She hugs Alex too. She wonders if he remembers asking her out when he was fifteen. As she pulls back, his pink cheeks suggest that yes, he does remember.

It's awkward. Usually, Noah is the conversationalist. He asks about things people would have forgotten about, like if Alex is still enjoying football camp and if Patrick got a good grade on the art project he tried so hard on.

But now, he stares at his drink as Olivia leans on the windowsill next to him. She's careful not to touch him at all, even if every part of her body gravitates toward him.

"How long have you two been together?" Alex asks, his gaze skipping between her and Noah. "I saw your stories on Instagram."

Oh. She's not sure how a fake breakup hurts this much, but her throat feels thick with it. She glances at Noah, and he looks as confused as her, and she hates that she doesn't know what he's thinking.

His mouth hangs open for longer than a second before he clamps it shut. He blinks rapidly before once again training his gaze on his cup. Olivia wrings her hands together, and the lump in her throat only grows, stubborn as she tries to swallow it down.

She realizes all too late that Noah hasn't answered. The conversation almost moves on, the group in front of her smart enough to figure out the facial expressions and the lack of answer, but it's too late. She's already talking.

"A while." She smiles. Noah's head snaps up to hers, and she usually loves when he looks at her, but not now. Not with his brows furrowed as if she could really hurt him. Like maybe she already has.

"Cool," Alex replies, bobbing his head. Thankfully, as the silence drags on to near petrifying levels, Helen calls everyone to the table.

Olivia waits for Alex and Patrick to leave before turning to Noah.

"I'm sorry," she rushes out. "I didn't—I wasn't expecting the question, and I panicked, and—"

"Oli." He laughs, though his smile doesn't reach his eyes. "I don't mind being your fake boyfriend again."

"Do . . . Can . . ." She's thought about nothing other than what she would say to him if she could, and now he's right here and she can't get the words out.

"Let's eat," he replies.

The table is crowded, the food taking center stage. Everything looks divine, as it always does when Helen cooks, but Olivia knows she'll struggle to eat. She's sitting next to Noah, which annoyingly makes her feel both calm and like there's a live wire stuck under her chair. She can't tell if he's looking at her or if he's looking at what to put on his plate first. She doesn't know if he's going to ask her when she's finally going to tell him she loves him, or if he's going to ask her to pass the salt.

She doesn't move, waiting for the first round of people to take their food instead of risking having to ask someone to pass the mashed potatoes. Then everyone at the table will hear the shake in her voice.

She doesn't notice when Noah takes her plate, but he places it in front of her, loaded with a small amount of her favorite foods. There's no mint sauce. She's never liked mint sauce.

"Thank you," she whispers. She catches Helen's eye, and the heartbreak must be evident on her face, because she watches Helen swing her gaze between her and Noah. She watches her figure it all out. Olivia isn't even sure Helen knew they were fake dating, but she knows Joe realized she liked him.

"How did Noah finally land you, then?" Patrick asks jokingly.

She huffs out a laugh, her voice barely above a whisper, scratchy as she squeezes her fingertips against her glass. She can see the tension in Noah's shoulders and hands as he tries not to crush the can he's holding.

"He's my best friend."

"What are your plans for the weekend?" Helen frantically asks the table. She'll always get them out of tricky situations. (Once, when Olivia was seventeen, she went to a party without Noah—because he was annoying, and because she forgot he was the one who made her feel brave enough to talk to people she didn't know—and she had the beginnings of a panic attack in the bathroom. She texted Noah, and he came to get her six minutes later, climbing up the trellis and into the bathroom window when she couldn't get herself to unlock it. And when she got downstairs to the garden, Helen was waiting in the car with a blanket.)

Liv's gaze flicks to Noah involuntarily, but he's not looking at her. She's not sure why she thought they might do something for her birthday tomorrow. She doesn't care about birthdays. She never has.

The last time she saw both of her parents on her birthday, she was eight, and the last time she saw either of them was her seventeenth birthday. Kind of. She saw her mom a few days later, but she did bring a gift and an apology, so she lets it count.

She never told anyone at college when her birthday was, always saying it had been through the summer when everyone else had gone home.

"Er, I'm spending the weekend at Greg's," Noah says. And oh. Liv had forgotten about the beach house. It's not really what she wants to do for the weekend, but she did say she'd be Noah's fake girlfriend, and the thought of not doing that makes her heart hurt.

She opens her mouth to ask when she should be ready, but Noah beats her to it.

"I'll tell them we broke up, don't worry." He forces out a laugh. "I won't make you join us."

She never thought she'd be dating Noah, but now, that's all she thinks about, the last few weeks blurring the lines between what she thought was real and fake. She never imagined she'd be breaking up with him either.

It hurts, even though it was fake all along.

She swallows, forcing her hands to be steady. Helen notices, but she thinks the rest of the table is unaware that her heart is breaking in front of them. She's wanted to fall apart for days, but not here. Not right now.

Still, she can't help herself, and she asks.

"Did—er, did Beth ever break up with what's-his-face?" Olivia asks.

"Yeah."

She nods. Olivia can't be too mad. Noah will be happy, and that's all she ever really wanted.

CHAPTER THIRTY-FOUR

After dessert, Olivia says her goodbyes and leaves. She walks home alone, which should be fine because it's only next door, but she hasn't taken the walk by herself since she got back.

She's greeted in her apartment by the click of her front door closing. The air conditioning has been on for the past half hour, the notification brightening her phone at the table. The cold air does nothing to lessen the burning in her lungs. The apartment looks different today, in the dark. She lets it stay that way—not wanting to turn the lights on and see the discarded blanket Noah used the last time he was here.

She kicks her shoes off, then releases a shuddering breath that feels a lot like her entire body is about to fall apart at the seams. She digs her nails into her palms, attempting to cling to her last shred of calm. But as she lays on her bed, the faint smell of Noah's cologne invades her senses, and the first tear rolls down her cheek. Her throat burns as she tries to choke back a sob, but it's futile. She buries her face in the crook of her arm and lets it consume her.

She's not sure how long she lies there, holding herself as she cries, but she's jolted by the thud of Noah's door closing, the sound echoing through her mind.

Somehow, knowing he's back is worse.

It forces its way into her brain, a foul reminder of how he could be here with her. How he could be closing the door to her bedroom, but he's not.

She gets up, wipes her eyes, and changes her clothes. If she forces herself into sleep clothes, she'll fall asleep, and she won't have to hear Noah packing to leave for the weekend. She pulls the covers over her head, dragging her phone under with her.

It's just after midnight. Officially her birthday.

There's a rustling on her fire escape, and honestly, she's not in the mood to scare off any trash critter that made its way up six flights of stairs. But then there's a knock at her window, and she's a little tired but still pretty sure that animals can't knock.

It's not a woodland creature, and she's like sixty-seven percent sure it's not a murderer, because who would even knock? But still, it's midnight, and she's in a sleep shirt that's not even hers, so she gets up slowly.

"Oh," she whispers to herself when she sees Noah crouching outside her window. She rushes to push the window up so she can let him in. He usually lets himself in and the fact he waits for her makes her feel like she's made of stone. She's not sure why he's outside when she's pretty sure he's supposed to be getting ready for Greg's.

"Hey," he whispers when she opens the window.

"Hi."

"Can I come in?"

"Oh, yeah, of course." She stumbles over her feet as she moves back.

His feet hit the floor, but he has his back to her. She's about to ask him something lame like if he's alright, but then there's a small glow in her dimly lit bedroom, and he spins.

"Happy birthday to you," he sings, his voice low and quiet as he tries to ensure the candle doesn't blow out. There's a large cupcake in his hands. It's a little smushed, and she thinks maybe he made it himself, but if she thinks about that too much and the fact he's here then she'll cry. It's her birthday so she can cry if she wants to, but she pulls it back by the time he stops singing.

She blows the candle out. The only real wish she had is already standing right in front of her.

"Happy birthday, Oli," he says with a small smile.

She almost says it back—she's only ever able to be a dork in front of him—but she can't force her mouth to speak, the smile splitting her cheeks as he looks at her.

"Thank you."

He's close but not close enough. Like maybe he's not sure where he can be around her anymore, and that's on her. She hasn't reset the boundaries since they got blurred. Since he asked her to be his fake girlfriend and she fell in love with him for real.

She swipes her forefinger through the icing, licking it off her finger a moment later. Strawberry. She looks over at him, and the look on his face threatens to take her out.

"I texted my mom," she says, the admission making her head spin. She shuffles away, moving to sit on her bed until her back is against her headboard and pulling her knees up to her chest.

"Oh, yeah?" Noah replies. He places the cupcake on her desk and sits perched on the edge of her bed, his hands against his thighs. His clear unease makes her feel worse than her own mother ignoring her text on her birthday. (It's been her birthday for about four minutes, but track records show she will be ignored.)

"Mm-hmm."

She doesn't know how to fix it, though. She's always been on the other side. On the side of not knowing what you did wrong, of not knowing how to fix it. She's never thought about it from this side, and she doesn't like it at all.

"What did you say?"

"Oh." She laughs, the nerves getting the better of her. "Well, I needed someone to talk to—erm, about you."

"About me?" he asks, pushing himself further on the bed so he can face her. It's worse, she thinks, having his full attention. She feels the lump in her throat growing, and she blinks rapidly but it does nothing to stop her eyes from filling with tears.

"Well, I couldn't talk to Helen because she's your mom, and sure she helped me get over Ricky in sixth grade, but this is different, and I couldn't talk to Steph—well, um, I did talk to Steph, but she's biased—"

"Oli," he whispers, his hand against her ankle as she brushes tears from her cheeks.

"And the only person I wanted to talk about it with was you, but I couldn't because I—"

He pulls her ankle until she's close enough that he can wrap his arms around her.

"Don't cry," he mutters against her hair.

"It's my birthday," she replies with a huff, relaxing her shoulders until she's slack against him. "I'll cry if I want to."

"Dramatic, and for what?" he says with a laugh. She lets out a small sob—nothing too crazy—but she tightens her hands in his jumper all the same.

"You can talk to me about anything," he says, pushing her hair from her face. He wipes her cheek dry with his thumb as she looks at him. "You're my best friend."

"Yeah?" she whispers.

"Mm-hmm."

"You're mine too."

"I am?" he asks, wrapping her hair into a slack ponytail around his hand.

"Don't be weird about it." She groans, pushing him away, but he doesn't let her go anywhere. So, she rests her face against the crook of his neck.

"Oh, I'm going to be so weird about it," he says with a laugh.

"Why are you the worst?" she asks, smiling against his throat. She can feel his rapid pulse under her lips, and she takes a deep breath. She pulls back, swallowing as she chances a look at him. He's already looking at her.

She's kissed him numerous times, each time better and longer than the last, but it feels different now. The way his eyes drop to her lips as she swallows. He doesn't move; his eyes just flick over her face as she leans toward him. She figures he's always done most of the work, so she can do it this time. She moves closer, and he lets his hand rest against her ribcage as she breathes him in.

Her hands shake, and she thinks nothing has ever been as terrifying as this. No one in the world has ever been more scared than she is now, she's sure, but she needs to do it anyway. Her nose rubs against his and she parts her lips.

"I love you," she whispers down his throat. She presses her lips to his, but the kiss doesn't deepen, not with the way she can feel Noah smiling against her.

"I love you back," he says with a small laugh. "I love you right back."

The kiss is slow, soft, and everything she's ever wanted from him. His hand cups her jaw, his thumb tilting her face until the kiss deepens, and it takes all of her strength not to fall back against the mattress, pulling him with her. Instead, she slows down, her tongue stroking his as she pulls back because she knows she needs to say more, to tell him more, but with his lips this close she's not sure how she's supposed to tell him everything now that she could be kissing him instead.

She blinks her eyes open slowly, feeling like the stars in her eyes make up the universe, with Noah somewhere in the center of it all. He lets his hand fall from her face to rest against her thigh. She takes it because she can. Because he makes her feel safe in a way she never has before.

"I'm sorry—I'm sorry about the other day. I didn't—I don't know how," she whispers as she plays with his fingers. "I don't know how to let you love me."

He moves closer, pulling her legs until she's straddling him on the edge of her bed. His hands rest around her waist, his fingertips along her spine. She looks down at him as he smiles.

"Don't worry your pretty face about it. Just let me handle it, okay?"

Trusting someone with her heart is terrifying, but Noah has never let her down before. She leans down, brushing her nose against his as she breathes him in. His eyes are dark, his palms heavy against her back.

"Okay," she replies.

It happens quickly—the way his mouth crashes against hers, the feeling of spinning as she pulls at his hair. He throws her pillow on the floor, tilting her head toward the ceiling with his thumb under her chin as he kisses her neck.

"Noah," she pleads, though she's not sure what for. He'll give it to her anyway.

"You're so pretty," he mutters, pulling her lip between his teeth. "You've always been pretty."

"Oh yeah?" she asks, a smile on her face as he pulls back to look at her.

"You will always be the prettiest person in the room," he whispers, kissing her nose, her cheek, her lips. "And the smartest," he says, his lips against her shoulder. "The best, the funniest . . ." She can feel him smiling against her neck as she laughs.

"Shut up," she giggles, tilting her face to his.

"Never," he whispers. His hands pull hers above her head, holding them there. "I have decades to make up for."

"You don't have to make up for anything," she replies, her breath choppy as his grip on her wrists tightens. She leans up to kiss him, her fingers brushing along the backs of his hands. "As long as you like me now, I don't care."

"I like you so much," he gasps, slowly moving his hips. "I like you way too much."

CHAPTER THIRTY-FIVE

O livia isn't used to sharing a bed with someone, but she doesn't mind the effort of pulling her duvet back toward her because Noah is a hog. She doesn't mind the stiffness she feels in her back because Noah likes to be the big spoon with his arm thrown over her and he's too heavy for her to move. She certainly doesn't mind being woken up with Noah's lips against her shoulder.

"Birthday girl," he whispers when she stretches.

"It's barely morning," she groans, though she spins in his arms all the same.

"Grumpy birthday girl," he replies with a smile.

"You have to be nice to me. It's my birthday."

"You don't even like your birthday," he mutters, pressing his lips to her collarbone. "So I don't have to do anything."

"You're so rude to me for no reason," she jokes, threading her fingers through his hair.

"Mm-hmm," he says, kissing her shoulder as he moves down the bed. He looks up at her before he disappears under the covers. "I'll be nice."

Olivia takes another bite of blueberry pancake as Noah refills her glass with apple juice. The kitchen has some simple decorations that make her heart flutter. There's a small light pink balloon cloud on the kitchen island, and there's bunting across her living room ceiling and a pile of gifts she's trying not to look at. She's always liked decorating for events because she likes to make people feel special, as if their birthday is something that deserves pretty things. She's never admitted out loud that she might like it back, because it's so embarrassing when it would never happen.

But she felt a little overwhelmed when Noah walked her into the kitchen this morning. She's not sure if it's the confetti on the table or if it's just him. Maybe it's both. How lucky she is.

"I asked your parents if they wanted to do something," he says, his shoulders tense as she looks at him, "but they're fu—" He clears his throat. "They're not coming."

She shrugs. "I only want to spend the day with you." She hasn't thought about her parents today. She doesn't want to think about her parents today.

"Yeah?"

"Yeah. I missed you last year. I barely survived without my passive-aggressive gift from you."

"Don't be rude," he says with a laugh. "I've never missed a birthday."

"You know I haven't been here for three years, right?" she says, smiling at him as he takes a bite of her pancake. It's a little more than she'd usually have for breakfast anyway, so she lets him get away with it.

"I know," he replies, his hand against his forehead like a war widow. "The worst, honestly. But I sent flowers. That counts."

"They were from you?" she asks, her heart thumping like it wants to break out of her ribcage. She remembers the red carnation he gave her on their first fake date, and how they were the same flowers she received in college. She's not sure how she didn't figure it all out before.

"Of course," he says with a shrug.

"They never came with a card," she says. Olivia chews on her bottom lip as she thinks about asking him why. Maybe he never wanted her to find out. Maybe he didn't think she'd want them if they were from him.

He doesn't make her ask though, he just tells her. "You had to leave, " he says, quietly. "And I didn't want you to feel guilty about it. So, I didn't want to remind you of home too much."

Olivia takes a breath. A laboured, trying to keep her chest from heaving, breath. "Noah."

He smiles. The smile that she could see anywhere in the world and feel completely at home. "I thought you'd figure it out anyway, but clearly, you didn't know they were from me. So you get three extra gifts today."

"I don't want gifts."

"Oh, I don't care," he says, stealing another piece of her pancake.

"And I thought you loved me . . ." She sighs, feeling the happiness surge through her chest with the fact she can say it out loud, and the way she knows it's true.

"I do," he replies, leaning forward to kiss her on the nose. He takes her plate away.

"Hmph."

"Wanna go? You can grump about the gifts on our way."

"You're so annoying. How long do I have to get ready?" she asks, letting the excitement for her birthday flow through her veins for the first time in years.

"You're not going like that?" Noah asks, his brows furrowed as he looks her up and down. He seems to have forgotten he's also in sweatpants.

"Don't be cute."

"I can give you twenty minutes," he states, pressing his lips to her forehead, then he rinses her plate and places it in the dishwasher.

"Noah," she whispers, flicking her thumb as they walk out of their apartment building twenty-three minutes later. Olivia threw on her strawberry dress, some concealer, an unreasonable amount of blusher, and grabbed her bag. "Why do you keep going to hold my hand and then stopping?"

"Stalker," he groans, but it morphs into a laugh when she playfully shoves him. "I know you have a touching limit, and I don't wanna use it all up before lunchtime."

Oh. She knew he knew her better than anyone else, that he saw things no one else would ever be able to see, but she wonders if he knows her better than she even knows herself.

Not yet. Otherwise, he'd know she only ever wants to be touching him.

"Not with you," she mutters, pulling her lip between her teeth as he looks at her.

"Yeah?" he asks, his smile brighter than it reasonably should be at the fact she wants to hold his hand.

"Yeah," she replies simply. She leaves it another eleven steps before she reaches for his hand. He links their fingers together immediately, like he was just waiting for her to make the first move.

Even though it's her birthday.

Prick.

CHAPTER
THIRTY-SIX

"What do you mean?" Olivia asks. She's not sure where they're walking, but she's glad she wore cycling shorts under her dress and that she has her comfy sandals on. Noah made her wear a Birthday Girl badge because he's the worst (affectionately) and she said yes because she'd do anything he asked.

"Well, I said you could have three extra gifts, but it already took me weeks of research to find the *actual* gifts, so, instead of three subpar gifts, you get three wishes."

"Are you a genie?" she asks, swinging their hands as they walk down the street. It's a bright day, the gray skies of the past week leaving specifically for her birthday, she's pretty sure. Sure, it's the height of summer, but she's certain the sun is only out because Noah looks cute with shorts on.

"Maybe, but it'll cost you a wish to find out."

"Loser," she says with a laugh. Noah rubs his thumb over the back of her hand, and she feels content for the first time in a really long time. A comfortable silence falls over them. The only sounds she can hear are the happy squeals from children in the park one street over and the squawks of seagulls on the hunt for stray chips or ice cream.

Occasionally, Noah squeezes her hand, and she squeezes it back, and then he does it twice, and she repeats the action. It has her smiling at the ground, at the side of his face, and at random people in the street, because how can she not?

"Can I have your tote bag, please?" Noah asks.

"Sure," she replies. He already has his backpack, so she's not sure what else he's planning on carrying, but as she watches him smile at the flower stand in front of them, she figures it out.

"Gift number one is a cheat," he starts, slowing down when they're at the flower stall, "because you have to pick them. I have no color coordination."

"True." She laughs, but she likes his light blue shorts and blue top all the same. "But I like when you pick things. I like to know what you'd have chosen."

"Okay, I'll pick some *and* you pick some," he says. She watches him study each of the labels carefully as if he has any idea what they mean. Liv just picks based on which ones she thinks are pretty.

"What are you looking for?" she asks, walking closer to him. She doesn't think she could help either way, but she rests her hand against his. Maybe she just missed touching him.

"Um, mind your business," he replies, though he twists her fingers with his. "I wanted your birth month flower, but I don't think they do them. Even though it's August. Very rude behavior."

She smiles up at him, pulling him closer. "How do you know what my birth flower is?"

"I know everything about you," he whispers, kissing her quickly. "Or I googled it."

"Nerd," she breathes, letting her lips linger against his. She's going to pick carnations. Red ones.

"Go and pick some," he says, turning her to face the flowers. He drops his lips to her shoulder. "Please."

Olivia looks over the beautiful, colorful flowers in front of her. She's usually a bright white flower with green foliage girl, but she's feeling colorful today, so she grabs some red carnations and a few purple alstroemerias. She also picks up some white tulips because she always has white tulips.

She turns to ask him if this is okay, but all she sees is him, a potted plant resting between his arm and his chest and his phone out, taking photos of her.

"Stalker." She smiles. "What did you pick?"

"Oh," he says, looking down at his pastel-pink potted hydrangea. It's cute. Like him. It's also half-dead. Like her. "This doesn't really go with those, hmm. That's okay, we'll get these!"

He puts his potted hydrangea back down, takes the flowers from her, and walks them into the small flower store. It's flowers from floor to ceiling, buckets of single-stem roses and houseplants hanging from railings. She looks around, wondering if she should buy any to keep in her apartment—if she decides to stay there—as Noah hands them to the store assistant. Liv turns back to him because she's a loser and she loves him, but she catches him looking back at the sad-looking hydrangea a few times.

"You named him, didn't you?" She laughs, wrapping both her arms around his free one.

"I know it's your birthday," he starts, widening his eyes playfully at her, "but I will leave you here."

"Just get him!"

"No, he doesn't match your aesthetic," he says, looking at her flowers being wrapped flawlessly by the store clerk. They're so pretty. She loves pretty things, but if Noah only gave her half-dead plants for the rest of time, she'd be happy with that. Besides, he kept Larry alive for three years, so she thinks he can bring this one back from the brink of death.

"I want to use one of my birthday wishes," she says, her brows high as he gives her a stern look.

"Oli," he says with a sigh, but she's already gone. She grabs the potted hydrangea. It's light, showing how underwatered it's been—she guesses it was hidden by a bigger, better hydrangea—but it's a light pink with green edges, and she can't wait to see it live on their fire escape.

"Can we get this as well, please?" she asks the assistant. John. She looked at his badge but won't call him by his first name because it's creepy when people do that.

"Er . . . is that even alive?" he asks, swinging the pot around. Olivia thinks he should probably know that, seeing as it is his job to keep them alive, but she uses his confusion to knock the price down.

Noah places her flowers upright in the tote bag he borrowed from her, and he squeezes the hydrangea next to it. When he loops it over his shoulder, she can see the petals blowing lightly in the breeze next to his head, and she thinks maybe it's her favorite sight of all time.

She snaps a quick photo, or twelve, already thinking about the watercolors she'll buy so she can paint him later. She changes her background. She doesn't tell Noah.

CHAPTER THIRTY-SEVEN

Noah only makes her walk for about ten minutes before he points to a rare free space under a tree on the grass beside the promenade. One of her hands is wet because the raspberry lemonade Noah just bought her is melting and the outside is dripping with water droplets, and the other is *slightly* wet because she won't let go of Noah's hand even though it's thirty degrees outside. (The next time they move, she'll settle for a pinky link.)

He pulls a thin blanket from his bag, fluffing it out before he offers for her to sit down. Olivia is glad she wore cycling shorts under her dress because now she can sit however she likes, and she saved herself from thigh rub—the main reason summer days used to be ruined for her.

She pops her drink on the ground, taking Noah's from him as well. She sits down, waiting for him to stop shuffling around, but she doesn't mind—she uses the time to watch his thighs flex with every movement he makes. She loves him in shorts.

"If I don't use all three wishes today, can I use them to-morrow?" Liv asks between sips of her lemonade. It's good, but she decides everything tastes better on Noah's tongue, so she leans up to kiss him because she can.

"Well, I've never been able to deny you anything, so why start now," he mutters against her lips. "Also, you've only got two left."

"Oh, yeah! So, what did you name him?"

"Secrets," he says, pulling a small canvas cooler out of the bag. It's full of handmade sandwiches and crisps, and she loves him.

"How did you have time to make these?" she asks, peering into the box. But she doesn't hear his answer, her gaze dropping from the ham-and-salad sandwiches to the sweet red berries she sees just below.

"You got strawberries for me?" she asks, her face splitting into a smile as she sees the label from the store she loves.

"Of course. A birthday without strawberries? Not on my watch."

He unwraps the food and places it carefully on the blan-ket. The sandwiches rest on the beeswax wrap he attempted to wrap them in. Noah picks a strawberry up by the stem, inspecting it closely as if they've ever had bad strawberries from Mick's before. He pulls his water bottle top up with his teeth and rinses the strawberry with water before passing it to her.

"So," he starts. "What do you want to do now?"

"I don't—"

"Wait!" he shouts. She screws her nose up when a group of teenagers looks over at them. She's not sure what age she got to before a group of youth was suddenly terrifying. "Gift time."

"I want my braids back." Olivia sighs, running her fingers over the notebook Noah got her for her birthday. It's light pink and covered in cartoon Black women with braids and twists and afros, and she loves it. He also gave her watercolors, and she's resisting the urge to break them open now. She could—he bought her a new sketchbook, so she could definitely paint right now if she wanted—but she keeps getting distracted by his face, so she just looks at the colors and imagines which ones will make the freckles on his face stand out.

"Yes," Noah whispers from his space lying beside her. "You look so hot with braids."

"Oh, I do, do I?" she asks, leaning over from where she's sitting just to kiss him again.

"You're the loveliest in every room, ever ever ever. But yes, I do have a soft spot for the braids. I think." He twists one of her curls around his finger. "You with braids in high school was the first time I realized I thought girls were pretty."

"You thought I was pretty in high school?"

"Oli . . ." He laughs. "You've always been the prettiest person in the universe."

"The universe, huh?" she replies, swallowing as she looks over her gifts.

"Every universe," he promises.

"Mm-hmm." Olivia finally unwraps the sketchbook. It has a red material ribbon wrapped around it that she uses to tie the top half of her hair up. Because her hair is getting in her face, not because Noah likes it like that.

The sketchbook is a black faux leather and has her initials stamped in gold in the bottom right corner. She runs her fingers over the indentation. O.V.B. Olivia Violet Baxter.

"It's beautiful," she whispers. "Thank you."

"You're welcome," Noah replies, smiling up at her. She cracks the spine, breathing in as she opens it for the first time. She loves the smell of new sketchbooks, but as she does, a pencil drawing captures her eye.

It's her, she thinks. There's a borderline-awful drawing of two people. A sketch, really. But there are strawberries dotted around, and there's a faceless girl with box braids and a faceless guy next to her with curly hair and sunglasses the same as the ones Noah has perched in his hair right now.

"It's us?" she asks, her voice breaking as she looks at him. Noah hates to draw, but this might be her favorite piece of artwork she's ever seen.

"Yeah," he replies, his cheeks pink. "It's just on a piece of paper, so you can take it out without ruining the book—"

"Never," she says, pulling the book close to her chest.

"Well . . . I thought you might like to receive a drawing for a change."

"I'm so in love with you," she says, breathing heavily.

"If that's not the best thing I've ever heard," he replies, pressing his lips to her knee.

She's been thinking about it since the email came through—since she applied for the job, if she's honest—but she decides right here and now. She wants to stay here. She wants to take the job that means the most to her. She wants to decorate the apartment in shades of green, and she wants to get new plates and a new shower mat. She wants to live a life she's proud of, one that makes her happy. She wants to offer for Steph to come and live with her.

She wants to stay with Noah.

"I'm taking the job here," she says, flicking through her sketchpad. She runs her fingertips over the smooth bumps of the watercolor paper.

"Yeah?" he asks, his eyes wide. She can tell he's trying to act like he'd be happy either way, and it's adorable. She knows he would be truly happy if she was doing what she loved, even if it meant she was hours away.

"Mm-hmm. It's my dream job, so it just makes sense to stay here."

"Makes sense." He shrugs, then leans up to kiss her. "And it makes me very happy."

"Well, of course, your happiness at me being next door was the second reason on my list."

"You're staying in the apartment?" he asks, his eyebrows nearly touching his hairline.

"Yeah. I mean, you were right. It makes sense, even if it's only for a little bit. Maybe I'll get a roommate."

"Do you want my references now?" he asks, pulling his phone out of his pocket. "I have it on good authority that my mom would be happy to give me one."

"Do you promise to let me listen to Elodie every Saturday morning, even though I can't speak Italian and I just mumble along?" she asks. It's the most important question she has, only just edging out "Will you take the trash out each Tuesday?"

"As if I can't hear you from my bedroom anyway," he says with a laugh. "I love hearing you sing."

"Yeah?"

"Mm-hmm, and I wouldn't be mad at waking up with you. But . . ."

"But?" she asks, feeling her throat burn as she waits for him to say he doesn't want to live with her because she only told him she loved him for the first time twelve hours ago. Adults are always telling her there's no rush—she has the rest of her life to spend with him. But she feels like she's been waiting for him since she first learned what love was, and he was right here the entire time.

"I want to live with you," he states quickly, and her breathing settles. "But we can do it slowly if you want. I don't—I have loved you for longer than you know, and I don't want to mess it up by being—well, over the top, like I always am."

"I love you," she says, holding his hand, pulling him toward her slightly. "I love you exactly how you are."

"Oh yeah?" he whispers, crowding her space. She doesn't mind, even if it makes her feel too hot for an open, public area.

"Yeah," she replies. "Besides, there's still another room."

"Not you asking me to move in and then making me sleep in your parents' room." He laughs and rolls onto his back, crossing his ankles as he turns his head to look at her.

"I didn't even ask you to move in!" she replies, but he crosses his arms over his chest. "But you can, please—I would like that. I just meant with the slowing it all down . . . there's another room, for maybe another person."

"Oh, good idea! I have an idea—"

"And I know—oh, you have someone in mind?" she asks, thinking she already has the perfect person for the place, but she supposes she can talk to him about it first. He's only met Steph a handful of times, mainly on FaceTime and only once in person, but she has no worries that they wouldn't love each other.

"Steph!" he exclaims, sitting up and rummaging through his bag. "I mean, you said she just wanted to get a café job or something, right? Until she decides what she wants to do? She could do that here."

"Yeah," Olivia whispers, feeling like she's on cloud nine. He pulls a haphazardly wrapped gift from his bag, and she's not sure what else she could possibly need that would make today better.

CHAPTER THIRTY-EIGHT

"**I** have my next wish," she says as they walk along the promenade. They've done this walk together more times in her life than she can remember, but this time is her favorite. Her feet ache a little, and her hair keeps blowing into her lip balm because it's breezy this close to the sea, but her pinky is linked with Noah's, and she has an ice cream in her hand.

"Oh yeah?" he asks, the excitement evident in his tone and the way he practically skips so he's in front of her. They don't stop walking—Noah just walks backward with more ease than most people have walking when they can see where they're going.

She feels bad her wish isn't more exciting.

"What's the plant's name?" she asks.

"Oh my." He laughs, throwing his head back. He turns back so they're walking the same way again, then drops her hand, but he makes up for it by pulling her closer with his arm around her shoulders. He presses his lips to her temple.

"Harry."

"What's that for?" she asks.

"Because now we have one called Larry and one called Harry." He shrugs. He's the most ridiculous person in the world, and she loves him so much she feels a little dizzy.

"I'm telling Steph that," she replies, pulling her phone out of her pocket.

"You can tell her later," he says with a laugh, then, "She'll be here in a few hours."

"What?" Liv asks, stopping in place. Noah pulls her out of the way of a hoard of tourists as he spins to stand in front of her. "Steph's coming?"

"Well, yeah." He shrugs like it's no big deal. "You wanted to go to the arcade with Steph for your birthday, and it's your birthday."

"Noah," she says, blinking rapidly as he smiles at her.

"I know," he whispers, pulling her into a hug. "You can call me a stalker for remembering everything about you later when I beat you at Mario Kart. Well, actually, Dad's doing to beat us both."

"Joe's coming?" she asks, burying her face in the crook of Noah's neck.

"And Mom and Grams, but beware, Grams is unreal at the two-penny machines, so you better watch out."

"Thank you," she mutters. It's all she can do right now. He doesn't ask her for more.

"Wanna get tickets?" Noah asks, his fingers tightly woven with hers as they walk closer to the harbor.

The ferryboats are packed with people because it's nearing the evening. The promenade starts to clear out the second the sun begins to set, even if the sky stays a deep red and orange for longer than people think. It usually takes around an hour for the sun to completely disappear over the horizon, and she likes to take it in as much as she can. The boats have turned their lights on, and from this distance, they look like fairy lights around the sides.

"I'm not sure what there is to do over there," Olivia replies, her heart thumping in her chest. She's pretty sure he can hear it over the sound of the waves crashing against the rocks.

"That's alright," he says, and momentarily, her heart drops because there's never going to be a reason for her to use the ferryboat. But then he speaks again.

"We can just travel over and come back. We don't even need to step foot in the dark place. We've gotta be at the arcade in forty minutes anyway. But it's your birthday, Oli. We can do whatever we want."

"Mm-hmm."

"So, what do you think? Do you want to go on it with me?" he asks, turning to stand in front of her. His frame blocks out the low sun so she stops squinting, even with her sunglasses on.

She looks at him. The only guy that's ever had her back. The only guy she wants for the rest of time. The only guy that's ever wanted to give her the world wrapped up in strawberries and ferryboats.

"Yeah." She smiles. "I want to go on it with you."

Noah pays for their tickets, and she gawps at the ferry ride being four pounds seventy-five when it takes all of about five minutes and doesn't even land them in another country. But the thought blows away with the wind as Noah holds her hand, asking her if she wants to sit at the top of the boat or inside. Olivia takes a brief look at the inside, then steps to the side to let the people behind her find their seats. It's nothing bad—just rows of the cushion-lined seats she might find on a bus.

"Let's go up," she says, pulling his hand as she races for the stairs. They're steeper than she was anticipating, but the view from the top is worth the extra effort. They can see the entire town from up here, sort of. She can't see her apartment, but she can see the building, and the way the land gets greener as they get toward the sea.

Noah finds some seats, testing out a couple before he picks a two-seater off to the side. No one else comes up here, even as she hears the gates close. He places their bags down and then pulls her over to the railing. Everything is clear from the seats, but she doesn't mind standing because the angle is better for pictures.

When the ferry begins to move, she realizes the trip is cute but unnecessary. There's nothing she can see from here that she couldn't see from the ground. But it doesn't matter. It never did, not really. It wasn't about the ferryboat at all. She just wanted someone to follow through on what they said they'd do. And as she looks at Noah, his face close to his phone as he focuses on his picture, she realizes she has that person. The one who will say he'll pick up strawberries for her just because she wants them, even though they're nine blocks away, and he'll do it. The one who will say he'll take her to buy new stationery for her job next week, and he'll do it.

The one who will tell her he loves her. And he does.

That's all she ever needed. It's all she'll ever need.

But the ferry ride is pretty all the same.

"Next month, Dad wants to go on a hike."

"Where abouts?" Olivia asks, leaning against the railing.

"You know the trail near the woods we went to on residential in high school? You've got no excuse, because I know you don't work Thursdays," Noah says, pressing his lips against her shoulder.

"Noah," she warns. Hiking is not her forte. "I work Fridays."

"Mm-hmm. Take it off," he whispers, leaning his chest against her back. "I'll drive us up. You love a road trip."

"I do." She sighs.

"You love me."

"You're the worst," she replies, spinning around. Noah holds her hair out of her face, collecting it in a loose ponytail behind her back. He smiles at her.

"How small is the hike?"

"So small," he says, leaning forward until his lips are touching hers. "Practically a hill."

"Noah . . ."

But it's no use. He's willing to negotiate. He slides his tongue along her bottom lip as his hand tightens in her curls. She's going to stop him because they're on top of a ferryboat, even if the sun is setting and there's no one here with them. She's going to stop them but then she doesn't have to—he's pulled away. Olivia's breath comes heavier, her entire chest almost hitting her chin with the force of it all. The laughter that creeps out of her throat at the sight of

Noah chasing after the crisp packets that fell out of her bag do nothing to make her breathing easier.

She watches him run through the aisles, then disappear behind a bench. He pops back up moments later with the culprits in his hand, and she's surprised her cheeks haven't split in two with how much she's smiled today. He catches her watching him, and she screws her nose up when he winks at her. Olivia spins to watch the horizon. She knows Noah will catch up with her in a second.

There has never been a time in her life when she's felt so secure. When she felt like she could screw up and it wouldn't be the end of the world, someone would be there for her anyway. When she felt truly peaceful, even as her hair twists in front of her face and the birds chirp at the coast. There's never been a time when she felt like she was truly home.

She spins around to find him, because she misses the weight of his arm around her waist. It takes her a moment to keep the curls out of her face—the wind is determined to blind her—but she does it. He's standing next to their bags on the seat. She can see the edge of his smile behind his phone. He's taking photos of her.

"When I get a restraining order on you . . ." She laughs and throws herself against him. He catches her, as she thought he would.

"Is that your final birthday wish?" he mutters, pushing her hair from her face.

"Stay with me tonight," she whispers, kissing him quickly. "That's my wish."

"That's a bad wish," he replies, kissing from her mouth across her cheek to her ear. "I'd stay with you anyway."

"Mm-hmm," she replies, sitting on the seat next to him lest they get done for indecent exposure. There's no one else on the top deck, but still, the captain could call them out on it. She doesn't tell him she never needed three wishes from him—that he's the last good thing she'll ever need.

"Stay forever then," she says, her heart in her throat. It's a joke, sort of. She knows forever at twenty-four isn't something that happens all the time, but there's never been a time when Noah hasn't been on her mind. When she hasn't felt alive and cared for and loved in his presence.

"Forever sounds perfect."

"Loser." She laughs, but she leans against him all the same.

"Hey, it was your wish." He laughs too, his hand holding her hair back for her. They're silent for a while, listening to the horn of the boat as it pulls away from the harbor, taking them back home. She thinks her home is wherever Noah is. She won't tell him that, not right now. But she does miss looking at him, so she tilts her head.

He's already looking at her.

"Stop looking at me like that," she whispers, her eyes dancing between his eyes and his lips.

"Like what?"

"Like you love me."

"That's how I always look at you."

EPILOGUE

The train conductor announces they're pulling into the harbor station as if she wouldn't have noticed that this was her stop by the way it crawls along the coast. She doesn't mind, not tonight. She's on her way back from Steph's, helping her to pack the last of her stuff from her bedroom so she can hire a moving van next week. Her parents are refusing to bring her, but neither of them was particularly shocked that she was moving.

Olivia can't take the day off to do the drive with her because it's her first week at her new position, and she thought it would be a bad look to take the day to help her friend move. She wanted to—she already had her form filled in—but Steph threatened to not turn up if she risked her job like that. It's a little dramatic, she thinks, but Steph always has been, so she traveled up this weekend to help her decide what she should actually bring with her so they don't end up with four different pairs of straighteners and seven wax melts.

She was only gone for two days, but as she watches the waves out of the window and stands up to walk to the door, she finds she's missed home. She's been texting Noah all weekend like she's been sent off to war and not a few hours down the road. There should be an embarrassment seeping through her skin as she thinks about how often her phone buzzed with an "I miss you too" text, but she's refusing to let it break through.

The sky is darkening, the main tell that summer is coming to an end, and she sees the streetlamps flicking on. Olivia wishes she asked Noah to pick her up from the station, but it's still new. She's happy to tell him she loves him because she's not sure how to stop herself, but she's still learning how to ask for things from him. She's still working on letting him love her. She did text him when she got on the train, and she'll text him when she gets off because he likes to know she's safe.

He'll be there when she gets home, though. Probably with the kettle just boiled as he makes her tea and waters Larry and Harry. (They brought Larry into the house instead of leaving it to suffer through another winter—he's been through enough in his short life.) Noah's probably folded all the blankets and lit the candles they bought last weekend. He's probably making it feel like home, and that's enough. So, she watches the sea disappear behind the red brick train station with a smile.

Some of the flowers are still in bloom, the colors changing from vibrant to pastel, but they're beautiful all the same. Olivia grabs her bag from the seat next to her, stands, then runs her hands across her thighs to make sure her jeans aren't shoved up her bum on her walk home. She walks to the train doors, holding onto the handle as she waits for the train to stop, and she doesn't have to look at the station anymore. She can walk home looking at the sea.

Her view is better though when she sees Noah leaning against the wall, his ankles crossed. He looks up from his phone as the train pulls in, and he looks straight past her. Liv laughs when his neck almost snaps as he looks at her again. He's smiling her favorite kind of smile as he walks up to her train. He catches up with her, his pace easily matching the train's speed. She's never been so glad that it moves at a snail's pace.

His arms are behind his back, and he's rocking on his heels and she just wants the train to stop already. She thinks she can forgo a tea that's at drinking temperature when she gets home if she gets to hold his hand along the way.

The doors open, the breeze blows her hair into her face, and she feels entirely at home.

"Hi."

"Hey," he replies, pulling his hands from behind his back. He's holding a bunch of flowers, red carnations, and an A4 piece of paper that reads "Welcome back from prison."

Olivia throws her head back laughing as she steps off the train.

"I can't believe you."

Noah smiles brightly. "I aim to please."

He pulls her into a hug that she's all too willing to reciprocate. She breathes him in, and he smells like her place, and it makes her heart swell that he's there even when she's not. He takes her bag, and she gives it over because she'll lose the argument if she doesn't anyway. She swaps him for the flowers. He leans the extra couple of inches and kisses her. She trembles against him slightly, gripping his sweatshirt, but she doesn't mind. His lips return to hers firmly as she whispers his name, and she'd laugh if she had any breath to spare.

"How was your trip? Is Steph excited? Did you see any cows? Are you hungry?"

"Noah . . ." She laughs, and he stops asking her questions.

"Sorry." He smiles and rubs his thumb over her cheekbone. "Wanna go home?"

She wants to tell him that home is wherever he is. She wants to tell him she had a great trip, even if Steph's parents don't deserve her. She wants to tell him Steph is so excited and that she forewarned her about Noah's long showers. She wants to tell him she didn't see cows because it's too early in the year and they haven't been moved from the other field yet, but that's okay because she wants to see them with him anyway. She wants to tell him she is hungry, but they can make pasta together when they get home.

She wants to tell him they should get tacos and introduce Steph to Oscar next Thursday. She wants to tell him that she texted Joe asking if they could take the puzzle from his office to complete on Sunday (well, the next couple of Sunday's probably). She wants to tell him everything for the rest of time, if he only looks at her like this. But she has time. For right now, she just answers one question.

"Yeah," she mutters, taking his hand. "Let's go home."

The End

About The Author

You can find **J.S. JASPER** on the following:
Instagram @jsjsprwrts
Tiktok @jsjsprwrts
Twitter @jsjsprwrts

Printed in Great Britain
by Amazon

25487612R10169